LAWLESS

Tracey Ward

TRACEY WARD

CHAPTER ONE

My skin feels tight. It's sticky from the dried salt water of the sea, burning from the heat of the afternoon sun that touches on every inch of bare skin it can find. My swimsuit will smell like the ocean for days. I won't wash it. I'll take it with me to Boston and I'll let it smell like California. I'll let it remind me of today. Of my last day.

"They're setting up a bonfire," Katy comments.

I roll my head to the side, squinting one eye open to see the group of six guys gathering firewood down the beach. It's the surfer crowd. The ones who get here at dawn and don't leave until well after dark. They live here because they live for the ocean. For the waves and the crash and the ride. Their bodies are toned from the sport, browned by the sun, their hair bleached out with natural highlights that most of the girls out here would pay a fortune in the salon for. There's a handful of them, all hot and smiling, but one stands out. One always stands out, no matter where he goes.

"Do you wanna stay?"

I close my eye and point my face up to the fading sun. "I don't know," I mumble to Katy.

"Do you still need to pack?"

"I've been packed for over a week."

"That eager to leave, huh?" she chuckles, but

she doesn't think it's funny.

Neither do I.

"Yeah, I guess."

I've lived my entire life in Southern California. I was born and raised in the small coastal town of Isla Azul parked about an hour up the shoreline from Malibu. Katy and I have lived next door to each other since we were born. I've been going to college at Santa Barbara twenty minutes to the north, and when I graduated high school I went with Katy and three other girls to Mexico to celebrate. It was the farthest from home I've ever been.

That will change tomorrow. Tomorrow I'll get on a plane that will take me over halfway across the country to Boston, Massachusetts where I'll study music at the New England Conservatory. It's a huge deal. It made the front page of Isla Azul's tiny little paper. My dad framed it and hung it on the wall so we could see it every day. So I could be reminded of where I was going.

Of the ticking clock running out on the life I've always known.

"We should stay then," Katy tells me decidedly. She lays back down on her towel next me, fanning her long brown hair out above her head. "We'll soak up the last of the sun. Send your butt to Boston looking tan and hot. Give those pasty white east coast girls something to be jealous of. Show 'em what a real true California blond looks like."

I smile, but I don't respond. I close my eyes, listen to the sound of the waves, embrace the burn of the sun, and I reach out my hand until it brushes against hers. Until she lifts her pinky, wraps it around mine, and I lock them together tightly.

It's another ten minutes before I can't take the heat anymore. The sun is going down but the summer is just getting started, just heating up, and that warmth is embedded in my skin. It's getting dark but there's enough light for one last swim. One last kiss of the crisp ocean cool before I say goodbye to it for an entire year.

Katy stays on shore, opting to go mingle with the surfers and scope out who's here. I know who she's looking for. They do too, and even though she's not going to find him or get any information about him, they welcome her with open arms. As I walk down to the water I see Baker hug her firmly, draping his arm over her shoulder while holding a beer loosely by the neck in his other hand. The other guys offer her a beer, nod in greeting, but I frown when I realize someone is missing. Just as much as Lawson Daniel's presence stands out, his absence does as well.

It shouldn't surprise me to find him out in the water. He's nothing but a dot on the darkening horizon, bobbing on his board with his legs dangling in the water, but I know what he looks like. Every girl in a hundred mile radius knows what Lawson looks like.

Sex and sun.

Golden brown hair and sea green eyes.

Sly smiles and broken hearts.

I've known him as long as I've known Katy and I'm more proud of the fact that I've never tangled with him than the fact that I got into the

NEC. I'm in the minority in both respects. Exceptional. Smart. Skilled.

Alone.

There's no one else in the surf when I step inside the waves. The white foam curls up frothing and eager over my feet, and I sigh as my body instantly starts to cool from the touch. Everyone else has gone up to the shore to find beer and food and other bodies. Everyone but Lawson and me. As I wade into the water I watch him sit patiently, waiting for the next big wave. The last one of the night. But unlike me, I know he'll do this again tomorrow. And the day after that. And the day after that. He and that board are as constant as the tide, as sure as the sun, and I envy him that. I wish more than anything I could have one more day. One last summer.

When I'm in far enough I dive down. I face a wave head on and I slip expertly beneath it, kicking hard to go farther and deeper. My skin aches with a burn I won't see until the morning when I'm getting ready to get on the plane. My flight will leave LAX before dawn and I bite down hard on a sob that tries to escape my throat as I realize I've seen the last of the California sun for an entire year. I won't come back at Christmas or Thanksgiving. My family can't afford it. Once I'm in Boston I'll be locked in. No room for doubts or reservations. No retreat.

I kick toward the surface, my lungs screaming for air, but once I give them what they want I go under again. Then again. It's not until I come up that third time that I realize I've gone farther out than I planned.

A wave crashes into my face, sending me down again, but I don't panic. I've been swimming this ocean since I was a toddler. I can handle it. I can take a wave to the face or a long swim back to shore. The key is to stay calm.

When I break the surface again I'm in the clear. The water is calm around me and I watch as the wave curls back toward the beach, lazily furling forward. I glance around, wondering if Lawson is still out here or if he took the wave. I'm surprised to find him paddling furiously toward me.

"Rachel!" he shouts, his voice barely audible over the distance between us. Over the rush of the wind and water. "Swim toward me!"

I frown. "What?!"

"Swim toward me! Now! Go!"

I shake my head, completely confused.

Lawson has spoken to me all of four times in my life. Once in elementary school to tell me I had a booger hanging out of my nose, once in middle school to say I looked good with boobs, once in high school to tell me he door dinged my car, and now out in the open ocean he's screaming at me to swim to him. His handsome face is pinched with anxiety and exertion as his arms dig hard into the water, propelling his body laid flat on his surfboard.

"What are you talking—"

Something brushes my leg roughly. I spin around, looking at the water to see what it was, but it's getting too dark. The glare of the setting sun is blinding me, making the surface like a mirror I can't look beyond. My heart races in my chest but I will it to calm.

It's probably one of his stupid friends, I tell myself. *They're probably playing a prank to scare you.*

Another touch. This time it hurts, like sandpaper dragging across my sensitive skin.

"Rachel!" Katy cries faintly from the shore.

I look back to find her standing knee deep in the water. Baker is holding onto her, holding her back from coming any farther in, and the look of sheer panic on her face tells me instantly that this is no prank. This is real.

I'm in trouble.

I turn toward Lawson and start swimming as hard as I can. I dig deep, pull hard, but he's so far. I wonder if I shouldn't have gone for the shore instead. It's too late now, though. All I can do is swim as fast as I can, hope he's doing the same, and maybe I can make it up onto his board with him before—

I go under. Something takes hold of my leg and yanks me down. The horizon disappears from my view in one sharp snap that brings my world to cool darkness.

Just as quickly as it takes hold of me it lets me go. I scream under the water, bubbles bursting from my mouth up over my face and into my hair as I struggle to get to the surface. I'm kicking hard and suddenly I ache in my right leg as my vision goes white around the edges.

My hands find air, leaving the water, but then I'm going under again. I'm going down and it's colder and darker than before, and even though my blood is screaming through my veins and in my ears, it's eerily silent.

Something takes hold of me under my arms. It pulls me in tight, pinning me to a mass behind me and I thrash and fight until I realize it's an arm. My hands find the hard corded muscle of a forearm across my breasts and I hold onto it tightly, desperately, as it pulls me upward. We find the surface and I gasp for air, pulling in water and oxygen and hope in big, heaving gasps that make my lungs ache in my chest.

My vision comes back to me in strange shades. The light is too bright, the shadows too dark. Everything is washed out and somehow too vivid at the same time. The sky is blood red, the water pitch black. The white surfboard phosphorescent bone.

"Grab hold of it," Lawson says breathlessly in my ear. "Can you lift yourself up?"

I reach for the board and I'm grateful when my body complies. I take hold of the opposite side and with the force of Lawson's hand on my hip shoving me upward I'm able to pull myself up until I can roll my body onto the board.

"Grip the front tight. Hold on."

I nod in agreement, my fingers hesitantly dipping back into the water just enough to wrap them around the gentle roll of the front of the board. Lawson's head disappears from my peripheral. It sends a jolt of panic through my body and I'm just about to sit up to look for him under the water when the board lurches forward. He's behind me, holding on to the tail end and kicking us back to shore.

I don't breathe the entire way. I'm watching for that iconic, telltale triangle to appear on the top of the water. I'm waiting for Lawson's strength to disappear below the surface. I'm waiting for the agonizing crush of mouth and teeth and nature to take hold of both the board and me, and drag us under again.

It can't take us more than a two minutes to reach the shore but it's the longest two minutes of my life. Lawson is relentless, his body unfailing as it wills us out of the water. Once he can stand he's running with me, his powerful legs plowing through the water. Thrashing loudly as people shout and he hollers back. Someone is calling 911. Someone else is getting a blanket. Lawson is calling for a knife.

The surfboard rolls and rocks in the water as he pushes me in. A wave crests and crashes over us. It jostles me. It nearly knocks me off the board but he's there, Lawson is there, his hands on me with hard certainty that keeps me afloat and pulls me back up onto the board. I grab hold of one of his hands with mine as my vision swims dangerously. The ocean, the sky, the sand, the sun, the stars – they swirl together in a sickening dance until I don't know up from down anymore. All I know is the hot pain in my leg and the gentle warmth of Lawson's hand.

"Stay with me, Rach," he says sternly. "Eyes on me, you hear me? Stay with me."

We've reached the beach. I'm on my back on the board, wet sand clinging to my face along with my blond hair. He brushes it aside so I can see him. So I can find him and his eyes, and I latch onto them as the world spins faster and faster.

"Is she alive?" Katy asks tremulously.

"Stay with me," Lawson repeats calmly, ignoring Katy. "Rachel."

"Stay with me," I whisper, my eyes full of his face.

He grins, relieved. "That's right. I need you to stay with me. Help is coming. They'll get you out of here."

I hold his hand tightly, afraid to let go. Afraid the tide will take me and I'll slip back into the water. Back into the darkness. If he leaves me I'll die. I can feel it.

I look at him in open terror, my heart in my throat. "Stay," I plead.

His grin fades as he nods seriously. "Okay. I'll stay with you. I promise."

I nod, feeling relieved.

Then sick.

I turn my head and vomit on the golden sand. It's all water. All ocean and fear that mingles in the foam of the surf and fades out into the ocean.

It fades to black.

CHAPTER TWO

"Rachel? Can you hear me?"

A light flashes across my eyes. It burns but then it's gone and there's nothing. Just the dark and the heavy feel of a weight on top of me. Pinning me down. I move to sit up but I can't. I'm under water again. I'm back in the dark in the ocean. I can't move my arms or my legs, I can barely lift my head, and I'm opening my mouth to scream when I feel the soft press of a warm palm against mine.

I can't see him, I can't hear him, but I know he's here. He promised me he would be.

"She's stable. Let's lift her. On three. One... two... three!"

I'm rising through the air. There's something solid underneath me and I think it's Lawson's board. I roll from side to side the way I did in the surf, but I'm steady. I'm strapped down tight, the rough scratch of a blanket painful on my burned skin. Sound changes, becoming echoed and hollow as I'm lifted high and pushed across the ground with a protesting *screech*.

His hand leaves mine and I grab for it, searching blindly. I open my eyes and lift my head, mumbling words that don't even make sense to me. It's dark inside, but to my right I can see instruments glowing. Panels and gauges. Controls. When the shadow beside them kicks on a switch the angry whir of an engine starts to vibrate everything around me. Someone holds the blanket down hard over my body as sand flies everywhere, making me close my eyes again.

"You can't!" a man is shouting over the roar of the chopper blades. "There's no room for you! We're taking her to Cottage Hospital! Meet her there!"

A needle goes in my arm. A mask descends on my face, oxygen filtering in and making it easier to breathe, but inside I'm panicking.

"Cut the bullshit, Chris!" Lawson shouts. "You know you can carry one more."

"Not you."

"I'm not looking for a joy ride!"

"It doesn't matter, man. You can't go with her."

"I promised her."

"You promise a lot of girls a lot of things."

"Oh, don't be a dick! This is serious."

"So was my sister. Now get the hell out of my way so we can take off! You're hurting her more than helping her right now!"

I hear Lawson curse angrily, but he doesn't fight the guy. I see it when Chris gets on board the helicopter, his shadow blending in with the rest of the darkness around me, and I wish I didn't have this mask on my face. I'd ask him to please let Lawson on board. I'd tell him I'm scared. I'd let him know what a bureaucratic asshole he's being.

"Wheels up!" the pilot shouts.

We rise into the air, leaving Lawson behind. Leaving Katy and the beach and the water. My body burns as I shiver under the blanket in a cold sweat and I wonder how bad it is. I can't feel my leg. It doesn't even hurt, but I know it should. It did before. So why doesn't it now? Is it because I'm in shock?

Or is it because it's at the bottom of the ocean?

***

I'm awake and alert when we make it to the hospital in Santa Barbara. They tell me it's a good sign. I ask about my leg, about how bad it is, and they tell me they're doing everything they can. No one lets me see it. No one tells me if I even still have it.

A team of men and women in white coats and scrubs meets us when we touch down in the parking lot outside the hospital. The stretcher I'm strapped to is lifted, legs kicked down, and they run me toward the Emergency entrance as the responding medics give all of my information to the hospital staff. Heart rate, time since the attack, location of the attack.

That's what they keep calling it; an attack. I don't know why but it sounds so weird. Like it's somehow not enough. Like that one word can't encompass the sheer terror and trauma of what it felt like to be pulled under the water against my will by something I couldn't see. Something I could never fight off.

One word can't possibly be all there is to

describe how it feels to barely make it out with my life.

I'm pushed down a hallway, through a bunch of doors, and into a stark white room. They change out the blanket draped over the top of me and the chill in the air sends me near convulsions. The room is freezing cold, even after they wrap my torso in a new, warmer blanket. A nurse wheels over an IV drip and injects the needle neatly into my arm. That I feel – the pinprick of a needle going into the tender flesh of my arm, but my leg is still missing. The nurse injects something into the IV, someone else secures the oxygen mask on my face so tightly the rubber straps pull at my face, and then the fog rolls in.

People come and go. The warmth is gone, then it's back, then it's everywhere and I'm nowhere.

I'm lost.

***

It's morning when I come to. The sunlight is pouring in through the window in the hospital room. I know immediately that that's what it is. There's no mistaking the stark white walls or the blue curtain pulled far across my right. I can hear a TV playing but I can't see it. I must have a roommate. I wonder what happened to them.

I wonder what the hell happened to me.

"Rachel?" my mom asks hesitantly.

She stands up from a chair in the corner, her face tight with concern. Her eyes guarded and hesitant.

"Hey, mom," I answer thickly. My throat is bone dry. My tongue is made of thick cotton.

She smiles, her body sagging with relief at the sound of my voice. "How are you feeling?"

I start to laugh at the absurdity of the question but it turns into a rough cough that won't stop. My mom quickly pours me a glass of water and I gulp it down in one long swig. I hand it back to her and immediately ask for more. This cup I take more slowly, enjoying the feel of the cool liquid on my throat.

"Where's Dad?" I ask.

Mom walks to the blue curtain next to me. She pushes it back to expose my neighbor – my dad. He's in his work clothes (coveralls and heavy boots) passed out with the TV remote in his hand and a juicer infomercial on the screen.

"He worked a double yesterday," Mom explains. "He was exhausted when we got here and then you were in surgery for hours and—"

"How many?" I interrupt.

She blinks in surprise. "Oh, um. I think it ended up being three total. It was after midnight before they brought you out."

My eyes flicker nervously down to the bottom of my bed. To the white blanket laid across my legs. To the two feet standing tall at the end.

I sigh in relief when I see them. "I didn't lose my leg," I breathe.

"Oh my God, no!" Mom cries, shocked by the idea. "No, not even close."

"Then what happened?"

"You don't remember?"

"I know it was a shark."

Mom's mouth pulls into a grim line. "A great white."

"Wow," I sigh, amazed by how real those words make it.

I never saw it. Until this moment, it was some abstract horror like a tornado or a tsunami. You know what they look like but you've never tangled with one up close. They're not really real until you do.

This shark bite just got real for me.

I lick my cracked lips, thinking. "I remember being in the water. I remember being pulled under. My leg hurt when I tried to swim away. Then... I don't really know." I look around the room like I'm looking for answers but I don't find any. Nothing that makes the memories make sense. "Was... was Lawson Daniel there?"

"Honey," my mom says softly, sitting on the side of my bed, "he saved you."

It comes flooding back. The arm across my chest. The hand holding mine. Green eyes and golden skin.

"He pulled me out of the water," I mutter to myself.

"He did more than that."

"What do you mean?"

Her face clouds, her relief fading into dismay. "The bite was high up on your leg. On your thigh. It nicked an artery. You were bleeding so fast. When he got you to shore he cut the cord on his surfboard. The one that attaches to his ankle?"

"The leash."

TRACEY WARD

"That's it. He cut that and tied someone's shirt to your thigh to apply pressure. The nurses said you could have bled out before help got there if he hadn't done it. They airlifted you out because of that cut."

I swallow thickly. "And the bite? How bad is it?"

"It's not pretty," she answers frankly, her face firmly serious. "They said you have chaffing on your lower leg where your skin hit the shark's scales the wrong way. You have a lot of puncture wounds up and down your leg. Some are pretty deep. Those are where he grabbed you to pull you under. But you're lucky. They think it was just curious, that it wasn't looking for something to eat. The doctors said judging by the size of the bite and what Lawson told them, it was a baby."

"A juvenile," Dad corrects groggily from my right.

I can't help but grin, glancing over at him. "Morning, Dad."

His blue eyes are open and on me, gauging me. Watching the way he always does. "Hey, kiddo. How do you feel?"

"Surprisingly good," I reply, stunned to find out that it's true.

I still have my leg and my life. The shark didn't take a bite out of my body. He didn't come at my arms or my hands, meaning I can still play piano. I can still go to the NEC.

Or can I?

"Oh, shit," I mutter, throwing my hands over my face. "I missed my flight to Boston."

"That's the last thing you need to be worried about right now," Mom scolds.

I drop my hands heavily. "But all that money. I told you guys not to get the travel insurance. Insurance that I'm sure would have covered shark attacks."

"It's fine. We'll be fine."

"Why would you need insurance?" I ask, regurgitating my own words in an oafish voice. "Nothing could keep me off that plane. It's a waste of money."

"You didn't know. How could anyone know this would happen? And besides, you don't need to worry about that. You need to worry about getting better."

"I am better. I feel fine." I look down at my leg, noticing the thickness of my right thigh under the blanket. The bulge of the bandages wrapped around it. "Why am I fine?"

"What do you mean?" Dad asks, sitting up and turning off the TV.

"I should be sad, shouldn't I? Or freaked out? Why aren't I freaked out?"

"Because you're high."

"I'm what?"

He points to the IV by the bed. The long, clear tube leading into my arm. "Liquid euphoria. You're so hopped up on painkillers right now we could tell you that your dog died in a fire and you'd laugh in our faces."

I scowl at him. "I don't have a dog."

"Are you sure?"

Mom swats him on the arm. "Stop messing

with her. She's been through enough."

"The good news is that she survived it." Dad looks at me seriously, his expression softening. "That's why you're fine, Rachel. Because you're alive. We're all fine, *better* than fine, because you're alive. Your leg will heal. You'll go on with your life because you still have one. Because you're still here."

He points at me with his thick, calloused fingers. The ones that will always be blackened by motor oil and hard work. That used to try to braid my hair when my mom was away and that smoothed pink bandages on my elbows when I fell off my bike. The fingers that taught me Chopsticks. That molded me into who I am today.

"That's *my* euphoria," he tells me quietly. "You breathing."

My eyes sting with tears I don't want to cry. I take a shaky breath and smile at my dad, so touched by the sweet sentiment of this rough, weathered guy.

Mom reaches out and takes my hand, smiling down at me. "We're both happy you're okay."

"Yes, we are," dad agrees, his entire manner shifting from sweet to stern in an instant, "because maybe now that you're awake you can explain to me why the hell Lawson Daniel of all people has been hovering in the waiting room demanding to see you all night."

CHAPTER THREE

He stands at the end of my hospital bed after a long, sleepless night. His eyes are puffy. His face is tired. He's wearing board shorts, flip flops, and a faded *Sublime* t-shirt, and yet he still looks like a model that stepped straight out of an ad for the female orgasm. It's not right. It's unfair, and it's every reason that I've been careful to keep clear of him all these years. But now there he stands – my savior. The man who just hours ago I clung to, pleading with him to stay by my side.

And the son of a bitch actually did it.

"Have you ever noticed, Lawson Daniel," I ask him slowly, "that everyone calls you by your full name?"

His mouth quirks into a wry grin. "Not until this moment, no."

"I have. I've noticed. Do you know why I think they do it?"

"No. Why?"

"Because you're trouble."

"That's probably true."

"My mom uses my full name when I'm in trouble. The same way people use your full name when they talk about you. Not like you're *in* trouble, but like you *are* trouble."

"What's your full name?"

"What's yours?"

"Lawson Daniel."

"What's your middle name?"

His grin grows into a smile. "What's yours?"

I roll my hand in a round-and-round gesture. "This is just going to keep going like this, isn't it?"

"Probably."

"I quit," I groan, letting my head sink deeper into the pillow, my face turning to the ceiling.

It reminds me of yesterday when I was laying on the beach. I was drinking in the sun, getting ready to start the rest of my life, and Lawson was nothing but a body by a bonfire. Just a name I knew. Now here he stands in the flesh and I owe him every breath I breathe through my body.

What a difference a day makes.

"I heard you're gonna be okay," he comments, coming around the side of the bed to stand by my right leg. He doesn't look at it, though. He only looks at my face. In my eyes. "No permanent damage?"

"Yeah. It'll scar, but they said I don't have any muscle damage. It won't hurt to walk. Not after it heals."

"When do you get to go home?"

"Tomorrow. They want me to stay overnight to make sure I don't have an infection. And I'll have to come back to get the stitches taken out."

"Couple weeks?"

"How'd you know that?"

He turns and shows me the back of his left leg. Through the thick brown hair I can see a white scar racing up his tan calf.

"Coral," he explains. "Ripped right into me. I had ten stitches."

"Where else?"

"Where else have I had stitches?"

"Yeah."

He grins again, turning to face me. "To answer that I'd have to strip almost naked and shave my head."

I roll my eyes. "Or you could just tell me instead of showing me."

"Scars are meant to be seen, not heard."

"Maybe another time, then."

"You know where to find me."

I do. Anyone who lives on this side of Los Angeles knows where to find him. On the beach. On his board. In the curl. He's been riding since he was a kid. He learned to surf back when the rest of us learned to ride bikes, but while we never got good enough to compete in the Tour de France, Lawson went on to win every amateur surfing competition he stepped into. I heard a rumor in high school that he was being courted by a sponsor. No one knew who but they wanted him to go pro, and they wanted him to do it wearing their label. It would have meant competitions in Australia, Hawaii, Brazil, Fiji, Africa. Even here in California. It was every surfer's dream come true.

A rumor is all it must have been though, because Lawson never left.

"I'll let you get some rest," he says.

He surprises me when he reaches out and lays a hand gently on my leg. My injured leg. It's soft and it's quick, like a pat on the shoulder, but something about the gesture touches me in a way I don't understand. In a way that's small like a pebble in a pond, just a ripple on the surface, but it will grow into something else. Something bigger, fuller. Into a giant, coiling, consuming mass of energy and life.

Unstoppable. Unforeseeable. Inescapable.

"Thank you," I tell him quietly, ashamed it's not the first thing I said to him. "For saving my life. Twice. Thank you."

He nods his head, his eyes on the ground. He's standing in profile, the light from the window pouring in behind him and draping his face in shadow. I can't read it. I can barely see it, but I can understand his stance. I can read his body language, and when he speaks, his words confuse me but they don't surprise me.

"Don't ever thank me again, okay?" he asks me, his voice surprisingly deep and vibrant. "I know you needed to do it once and I'll say you're welcome so that the conversation is closed, but I'd appreciate it if you never said it to me again. Can you do that?"

"Yes," I agree, though I have no idea why.

"Good. Thanks."

"You're welcome," I say sarcastically.

I'm relieved when he looks at me sideways, that iconic mischief in his eyes and a crooked grin on his lips. "I gotta go get some sleep. I'll see you later."

I nod silently, watching him go. He's at the door before I can't take it. Before the words are ripped from my throat because if I don't ask now

I'm scared I'll never get the chance.

"Why did you stay?" I call after him.

He stops at the door, one of his large hands wrapped around the frame. "Because you asked me to," he reminds me, "and I promised you I would."

He slaps his hand on the frame once and disappears down the hallway.

This short conversation is the most I've ever heard Lawson speak. There wasn't much said. There wasn't much about it I understood, but I feel like I see him more clearly now than I ever have before. Like walking a familiar beach on a foggy morning and seeing the mist start to clear by degrees. Watching it unveil the landscape you thought you always knew so slowly that you start to notice things you never saw before.

You start to see things for what they really are, not what you always thought they were.

CHAPTER FOUR

"Rachel!" Katy screams.

She rushes across the lawn, leaps over my mom's small rose bushes, and stumbles toward me. One of her sandals nearly slips off her foot, flinging her forward, but she recovers and barrels toward me without hesitation.

It's not until the last second that she slows enough to not knock me to the ground, but her hug is still bruising. It's crushing in its ferocity, pinning my crutches to my sides and making my ribs shriek in protest.

I could not care less.

"Oh my God, I'm so glad you're okay," she gushes in my ear.

I laugh, resting my head on her shoulder and leaning against her. I let her carry the weight she's stolen from my crutches and she takes it gladly. She knocks me down and holds me up all in one motion that's everything I didn't know I needed. I didn't know how scared I was until being home, until being with Katy, made me feel safe again.

She pulls back, her face stretching with a smile that looks like it hurts. "You can walk on it already?"

"The bone and my muscles are fine. I just have

to worry about my stitches for a while. I have to be careful not to tear them so the skin has a chance to heal."

She looks down at my leg, at the stark white bandages showing under my running shorts, and shakes her head in amazement. "I can't believe it. I had a nightmare about it last night."

"You saw the shark?"

"Just the fin. Xavier saw it and asked, 'Is that what I think is?', then Lawson was screaming at you and we all ran to the shore to call you in. You were so far out – I'm glad Law was there. He and his board were closer than the beach."

"Yeah, I'm lucky he was there."

"And hey," Katy says, nudging me playfully with her elbow, "if you've gotta be saved by a guy, might as well be a Daniel boy, right? At least they're pretty."

I smile encouragingly. "Yeah. They definitely are."

I'm worried she'll say more about it. That she'll break the promise she made to herself, that she'll say his name. That the floodgates will open and the world will be awash in her tears all over again. She's come a long way in the last year. She's stronger now. Smarter. I wanted to think she was moving on because I was leaving and I knew I wouldn't be here to help her, but now I'm not so sure. Thanks to the shark and Lawson and the fog that's lifting, I'm seeing things more clearly and when I look at Katy I see the pain. I see the doubt and the confusion, the longing. The hurt. It's never gone away. She just got really good at hiding it.

"You wanna lay on your bed, eat junk food, and watch a *Teen Mom* marathon?" she asks me suddenly.

"Dude," I say with dramatic relief, "you read my mind."

Snickers minis. Cheddar popcorn. Vanilla Coke.

This is how you recover from a shark attack.

This is how you heal a broken heart.

***

I fall asleep two episodes in.

Thanks, Percocet. Now I'm narcoleptic.

I wake up to find Katy gone and dinner on the table. It's still light outside, it will be until after nine o'clock, but I'm already thinking of my pajamas and getting back into bed. I want to sleep until the heat dissipates and wake up to roam around in the cool evening breeze rolling in off the ocean. The old air conditioner on the side of the house crapped out at the end of last summer and we suffered through the heat, saying we'd get it fixed before the season came back around again, but we never did.

We bought my plane ticket to Boston instead.

It's on my mind as I sit sweating at the table, watching my mom's blond hair stick to the nape of her neck. Dad grabs the front of his shirt every few minutes, pulling it away from his body and fanning the hot, stale air inside. Neither of them says a word. Neither of them will ever complain, and that's the part that kills me the most.

"I got an e-mail back from the law firm in

Boston," I finally speak up.

Dad glances quickly at Mom. "Oh yeah?" he asks me. "What'd they say?"

"They can't hold my job for me until the fall. They need someone now. They already called in their second choice."

"That was fast," he grumbles.

I shrug. "It's not their fault. They planned on me being there today. I couldn't follow through."

"Yeah, but—" Mom starts.

"It doesn't matter," I cut her off, knowing where she's going. "If I was having a baby, if I was dead on the side of the road, if I was drunk in a bar or laid out with a hangover – it's all the same to them. I didn't show up. I lost my spot. That's the end of it."

"What about in the fall when you're able to be there? Can't you apply again then?"

"The job was for the year. June to June. The person they pulled in today, they're staying all year. There is no job to apply for in the fall."

"It just seems so unfair."

"Life isn't fair," Dad says, speaking around a cheek full of pasta. His eyes are on his fork as he skewers more tubes coated in bright red sauce. "She can't work there this summer so she can't work there at all. We'll have to figure something else out."

"We'll buy you another plane ticket in the fall," Mom assures me.

I drop my arm to the table with a *thump*. "How? With what money?"

"We'll use the credit card."

"That's how you bought the first one. It's why we're all sweating balls in here instead of running the AC."

Mom sighs. "I don't ask a lot of you two, but can we at least not talk about sweaty balls at the dinner table?"

Dad lifts another forkful of pasta into his mouth. "Your mom is right, Rachel. Have some manners."

"While we're talking about manners, Rich, maybe you could stop talking with your mouth full."

"We gave you sweaty balls, honey. Don't get greedy."

"I never agreed to give up sweaty balls," I remind them.

Mom groans. "I'm ashamed to know you both."

"I was thinking about trying to get a job here."

The both pause, Dad with his fork venturing toward his mouth again and Mom with her hand fanning the back of her neck.

"Where exactly?" Mom asks slowly.

"I don't know. Somewhere close."

"It'd have to be," Dad says as though it's obvious. As though he's arguing with me rather than agreeing with me.

"What would you do?" Mom asks.

I shrug. "I don't know. Anything."

"Rachel, you can't do *anything*."

"I'm not crippled," I insist sharply.

"No one said you are, but you are hurt. You've been out of the hospital for one day. Give yourself time to heal."

"I don't have time!" I bite loudly, my patience evaporating in the oven we're living in. "I needed that job to make money to survive off of during the school year. Now I need to spend the summer trying to save up for another plane ticket on top of money for living expenses at school. I'll have to find another job during the school year in Boston, but I can't do anything about that yet. All I can do is take care of things here and that means getting a job."

"We'll buy your plane ticket for you. You don't have to kill yourself trying to make up that money."

"No. No more. Don't spend any more money on me. Spend it on yourselves for once."

I stand from the table, forgetting my leg and stumbling as it can't support my weight when I ask it to. I fall forward, sending the entire table rocking. Mom's iced tea spills. Dad's fork falls to his plate with a dissonant clatter.

All eyes are on me and I feel myself flushing with embarrassment and anger. With the heat of the house and the thickness of the air in my lungs.

I grab my crutches from the wall behind me and I hurry out of the room as fast as I can.

They let me go without a word.

I meant to go into the front yard. To get outside and see if I can taste the ocean on the air, but I can't. The world is still, the branches on the trees hanging low and tired. Lazy. Stagnant.

I pull my keys from my pocket and fumble my way into my car, kicking the AC on high immediately. When I go to the push the brake to kick it into reverse I whimper. I nearly cry out at the scalding pain the movement rushes through my thigh, but still I do it. I release it blissfully, gently tap the gas, and back out of the driveway before my parents can stop me. I'm on painkillers and I can barely use my right leg – I should not be driving. But I can't stay in the house another minute. Two days ago I was nearly brought to tears over the thought of leaving it. Now I'm dying inside having to stay.

I have no fucking clue what's wrong with me.

I start using my left leg to drive. It's weird and I have to focus hard to do it, but it helps. It makes it easier and luckily Isla Azul is not a big town. Six blocks gets me on the main strip. A quarter mile to the south lands me in the Frosty Freeze drive-thru getting my hands on a strawberry milkshake. Whatever that shark cost me in blood, I'm going to gain it back in fat, and then some.

Where to go next leaves me stumped. I don't want to go home. I don't want to be inside the Frosty Freeze, or even in the parking lot where people can see me. Everyone in town knows about what happened. Everyone will want to talk about it. I just want to eat my ice cream in silence, think about what a colossal mess my life is, and listen to some whiny music.

I find myself at the ocean, but it feels more like the ocean found me. Like it was waiting for me. Like it knew I was hiding from it before I did, but now that I'm here I know; I want nothing to do with it.

I don't even roll down my windows like I used to. I was looking for the smell of it on the air earlier but now that I know I can find it, I don't want it.

Just sitting in this parking lot looking out over the lonely stretch of empty sand leading down into the dark horizon has me shivering, goosebumps popping up over every inch of my skin. My leg aches like it's on fire. Like it remembers.

Knock, knock!

I scream, jumping about a foot in the air as my heart explodes in my chest. Someone's knocking on my window. Some soulless piece of shit who just scared an already freaked out girl out of her mind and looks an awful lot like a soaking wet Lawson Daniel.

"You okay?" he asks, his green eyes eerily dark.

I roll down my window, my skin still popping and prickling with adrenaline. "You scared the hell out of me," I accuse breathlessly.

He smiles. "Sorry. I thought you saw me walking up from the beach."

"No. I was kind of zoned out."

I look at him, *really* look at him, and see that he's in the same swim trunks he was in the last time I saw him. No shirt this time. Just his chest, sculpted and smooth with a thin peppering of golden brown hair that gets lost in the color of his skin.

I frown when I see the board under his arm. "You were surfing?"

"Yeah. It's too hot to be doing anything else."

"Out here? After what happened?" I ask incredulously.

He stands up straight, taking his face out of my window and replacing it with his abs. His six pack, glistening abs.

He's doing this on purpose.

I shove my door open and force him to step back. He watches me stumble out of my car but he never asks if I'm alright or makes a move to help me. That right there, it takes a little of the fire out of my veins. It restores some small measure of my pride.

He's doing *that* on purpose too.

I knock my door closed and lean back against it, blissfully relieving my leg of any strain. I nod to this surfboard tucked under his arm. It's blue and yellow. Not the white that I remember. "Same beach, same shorts, but a different board at least?"

He nods his head and turns his back, moving across the parking lot toward a black Subaru Outback. It looks brand new and since I've never known Lawson to have a job, I'm guessing his dad bought it for him. The Daniel family is the wealthiest in Isla Azul, though that's not saying much. They'd barely be upper middle class in any big city in California, but compared to the rest of us they're the Rockefellers. Alan Daniel has owned a boat dealership in Santa Barbara since before I was born. It's almost a half hour away but he grew up in Isla Azul and apparently he never plans to leave. It's a common mentality here. Contagious even.

Lawson lays the board on the rack across the car's roof, snags a water bottle out of the back, and saunters slowly toward me. His feet are bare. They probably are most of the time. The hot sand, the rough coral – they don't mean anything to him anymore. They're as comfortable as carpet on his tempered Hobbit's feet.

"I retired Layla," he tells me before taking a sip of his water.

"Your board's name was Layla?"

"Yep. She was one of my favorites, but she's done. I hung her up for good."

"Hung her where?"

"Should you be out driving?" he asks, gesturing to my car behind me and neatly changing the subject. "You got out of the hospital today, right? I don't think you're even supposed to be walking on that leg. Definitely shouldn't be driving."

"Probably not, but I had to get out." I glance out over the dark water, another shiver vibrating through my blood. "I regret it now though."

"Thinking about going in?"

I snap my eyes to his, stunned by the question. "No. Are you crazy? I almost died out there."

"One out of how many times?"

"Excuse me?"

"How many times have you been in the ocean," he points to the water behind him but keeps his eyes locked firmly on mine, "*that* stretch of ocean, and come out of it just fine?"

I shake my head. "That's not the point."

"It is, though. How many? Hundreds? Thousands?"

"I'm not you. I have interests outside of the ocean."

"Okay, so hundreds. You've been in that water hundreds of times and one of those times things went south. *One.* What's your favorite food?"

I chuckle in surprise. "What's my favorite

food?"

He takes a step toward me, lowering his voice but raising his lips in a small smile. "Do you answer every question with a question?"

"Do I—No."

"What's your favorite food?"

"Chicago style pizza. Stuffed crust."

"If Chicago style pizza with stuffed crust gave you food poisoning *one* time, would you never eat it again?"

"Does it land me in the hospital?"

"Yes. But you're out recklessly eating and driving again within a day."

"I'm not reckless driving."

"Would you eat it again?" he pushes.

"I don't love the ocean the way I love pizza," I answer him seriously. "I don't love it the way you do. I could forgive pizza. I can't forgive this."

He nods his head, his face falling to the ground the way it did in my hospital room.

"I get that," he says, his voice low. Earnest. The wind tries to take it, the roar of the ocean tries to steal it from my ears, but I find it. I grab onto it and I hang on his words. On his lips. "It's not about loving it, though. It's about overcoming it." He looks up at me, his eyes intense. "It's about not being afraid."

"Why do you care?" I ask softly.

"Because I've seen what fear does to a person. You let it win once, even a little, and it starts to take over. Just a little more and a little more until you're scared of everything and everyone. I've seen guys out there on the water who were fearless, but one wave takes them down and rattles them and suddenly they won't go after it like they used to. They're tourists. They take the easy way on everything until they don't even bother anymore."

I glance between him and the water, shifting on my feet and wincing at the pain it gives me. "Are you afraid of anything?"

He laughs, coming to lean against my car next to me. I can feel him. His body close to mine, the bare skin of his arm brushing against the bare skin of mine. He smells like the sea. Like salt and sun. Like everything I wanted to bottle up and everything I'm dying to get away from. That's Lawson to a T. Alluring and terrifying. Beautiful and dangerous.

"Everyone is afraid of something," he tells me lightly.

"Okay, so what are you afraid of?"

"Ghosts."

"I'm serious."

"So am I," he says, but his smile says he's anything but.

Whatever window was open for viewing into Lawson Daniel, it's closed now. He's shut it up tight, replacing it with the suave bravado the world has come to know and love so well.

"Let me drive you home," he says softly, his face surprisingly close to mine. "I wanna make sure you get there safe."

He's leaning toward me, his arm firmly pressed against me and his eyes baring down into mine.

Whoa, when did that happen? I think, instantly going on high alert.

I back away, leaving him leaning into the wind. "No, I'm good. Thanks."

"Are you sure? 'Cause you just about cried right then when you put weight on that leg."

I open my door, already falling inside. "I'm good. I figured out how to drive with my left foot. Thanks, though."

I go to pull my door closed but he grabs it above the window, holding it open.

"Hey, Rachel."

I sigh before looking up at him. "Yeah?"

"Remember what I said about fear, okay?"

"I will. But I'm not afraid."

He grins wickedly. "Not of anything?"

He knows why you're running away, idiot. He knows why women do all *of the things they do around him.*

"Lawson Daniel," I say breathily, my voice barely above a whisper, "can I be real with you?"

"You can be anything you want with me, Rachel Mason."

I lean half out of the car, putting my face within inches from his. My breath rebounds off his lips, coming back to me smelling sweet. Like strawberries and ice cream.

"Given the choice between you and the shark," I whisper, "I like my odds better with the shark."

I yank my door closed, forcing him to stand up and step back. I can hear him laughing as I put my car in gear and back out of the parking lot. I don't look back as I pull onto the coastal highway. I try not to think about the smell of him, the feel of him, his kindness and concern or the fullness of his laughter. I've nearly got him out of my head entirely as I pull into my driveway.

As I catch sight of a dark Subaru cruise by in my rearview mirror.

CHAPTER FIVE

"Hey, shark bait, what's shakin'?"

"No," I answer severely.

Wyatt chuckles, leaning his hands against the counter. His white Frosty Freeze ball cap is sitting high up on his head, his mop of black hair curling down around his forehead under the bill. The dark tendrils are wet with sweat, the heat from the grills in the back probably baking him as much as the summer sun was killing me outside.

"No to what?" he asks me, smiling easily.

"No to the nickname." I hobble toward him, resisting the urge to plop down in any one of the chairs I pass along the way. "No to talking about it. No to being known as the girl who nearly died by shark."

"What do you want to be known as?"

"The girl who got out of town, which is why I need to ask a favor."

"Anything, shar—malade. Sharmalade."

I tilt my head at him. "Really? That's what you're going with? That's your save? Sharmalade."

"I'm sticking to it."

"Cool. Anyway," I slide my resume onto the counter toward him, "I need a job and nowhere is hiring. This is my last resort."

"Flattering," he deadpans.

I wince apologetically. "I'm too hot and too tired for flattery, sorry."

He smiles faintly. "You want an ice water?"

"Can I bathe in it?"

"Can I watch?"

I laugh, instantly changing my tune. "I'll take it in a cup."

He fills a cup halfway up with ice and injects a quick stream of water inside before lidding it and handing it to me. I've never tasted anything better in my life.

"You been out in this heat all day?" he asks me.

"Ugh," I groan, setting the cup down. "The last *two* days. I've been applying everywhere in town but nowhere is hiring. The high school kids snatched up all the part-time jobs."

"Yeah, I know. We have three of them here." He turns his head toward the back, raising his voice. "Little assholes too!"

"Douche!" someone shouts back from the fryer.

Wyatt shakes his head in annoyance. "I hope that fry oil burns his dick off."

"Wow," I whisper.

"Yeah, see? You don't wanna work here. It's no place for a lady." He smirks, looking me up and down. "Or you."

"Fuck you," I chuckle.

"I take it back. Maybe you'd fit right in."

I sigh in exhaustion, sliding onto one of the stools lined up in front of the counter. "I don't want to work here. I don't want to work anywhere in Isla Azul. I'm supposed to be in Boston by now running errands in a law firm and making above minimum wage. Now thanks to this," I gesture disparagingly to my mangled leg, "I'm trapped here and I can't even get a job selling ice cream for eight bucks an hour."

Wyatt grimaces sympathetically, his face going serious. "You'd be on your feet all day here. You barely made it across the dining area without collapsing. You winced the whole way."

"Did I really?"

"Whole way," he repeats.

"I've been trying to go without the crutches. It's been a week, I thought I was getting better. I thought it made me look more dependable to be without them. Sturdier."

"It made me want to jump the counter and carry you just to make it stop."

I smile at him, my eyes softening. "You're sweet. You've always been sweet."

"You wanna tell Katy that for me?"

"I'll try, but you know how she is. She's still hung up—"

He reaches out and touches my hand, shaking his head. His mouth forms a firm line, his eyes shouting at me to shut up. To not say the name.

That can only mean one thing – Lawson is nearby.

My body responds immediately, my eyes dying to seek him out. The reaction worries me. I want to be strong, but right now I'm so tired and so weak I think I'm transparent. I'm a jellyfish – spineless. Listless.

And the currents keep pulling me toward *him*.

"I better get going," I tell Wyatt, standing quickly and gasping as I do.

He instinctively reaches out across the counter to steady me but I smile and wave him away.

I tip my drink toward him. "Thanks for the water. And for listening to me bitch."

"Take it easy, Sharmalade."

"Yeah," I chuckle, "you too."

I run from the Frosty Freeze. Well, okay, I don't run, but I bolt as fast as my cripple ass will carry me. I put on blinders, I keep my head down.

The heat hits me hard in the face and lungs when I make it out the door. It's hard to breathe for a second, transitioning from the dry cold of the AC into the humid heat outside. I take a slow, sluggish breath before I start across the blacktop. Heat rises off it in shimmering waves that play with your eyes and mess with your perception. The world roils and rolls around you like you're walking through invisible fire.

Or you're headed straight into it.

"Rachel."

Shit dammit.

He's in the shade at the side of the building. The long brick wall behind him is painted white but it's chipping. It's cracked, the multiple thick coats of color giving way to reveal a crimson fissure running from the sidewalk to the roof. Long and jagged. Like a scar.

Lawson leans against it in a pair of gray cargo shorts, a blue T-shirt, and a black baseball hat pulled down low over his eyes. The shadow cast by the bill makes it impossible to see him clearly, but I can feel his eyes on me.

"What?" I ask him curtly.

He grins with only half his mouth. Sexy and slow. "You having a bad day?"

I point impatiently to my leg. "I'm having a bad summer, Lawson. What do you want?"

"Just sayin' hey," he drawls.

"So I can go now?"

"You can do whatever you want, Rachel."

"Thank you," I say, turning on my good heel. "I'm going home."

"Rachel."

I sigh, looking back at him. "What?"

"Have a good day, Rachel."

"Why do you keep saying my name?"

He shrugs. "I've never really used it before. I get a weird little rush when I say it out loud." He pauses, watching me intently. "Do you feel that way when you say my name?"

"No."

He chuckles, dipping his hands into his pockets and leaning his head back against the wall. "That's a lie. Do you know why I think we get excited about each other?"

"Is this going to be a long speech?" I ask, pointing to the sky. "Because I didn't bring any sunscreen."

"It'll take as long as it takes. Longer if you don't play along."

"Or I could go home and it'll be over before you know it."

"You could, but you'll wonder all night." He takes a long dramatic step to the side, dragging his body across the wall behind him until he's standing at the base of the fracture, the red erupting from his shoulder up toward the sky. The sight makes me uneasy.

"Come stand in the shade with me," he offers.

I shake my head, holding my ground. "No, I'm good, but for my skin's sake tell the story quickly."

"That's just it. It's the story. It's because we didn't have one before. I didn't know you. I knew *of* you, but I didn't know *you*. Don't you think that's weird?"

"Not really."

"It is. This town is smaller than an ant's ass and I've got a story with every girl in it in one way or another. Even Katy and I have shit in common. But not you. Not until that night."

"I'm exciting for you because I'm new."

He smiles at me lazily. "Maybe. Or maybe I like the start of our story. Maybe I want to see what the rest looks like. Don't you wanna know, Rachel? Don't you wanna say my name and feel that feeling? That rush?"

I do. I absolutely do because I'm human, it's been months since a guy has gotten close to me, and dude is hot.

He's also high.

"How much have you smoked today?" I ask him bluntly.

He laughs, lowering his head until I can't see his eyes anymore. Until his entire face is hidden by his hat. "Yeah, alright," he mutters deeply. "I'll see you later."

I stand there, doubtful. Waiting, but for what I

don't know. I'm pretty sure I just got the brush off, though, and weird as it was, I take the opportunity to run. I head for my car, fall inside, and leave the Frosty Freeze far behind.

CHAPTER SIX

I have to expand my job search to Santa Barbara and Malibu. The drive will suck and I'm not so sure my leg can take it for the first couple weeks, but I have to try. I can't just sit in the house on my ass watching the summer tick away as my bank account dwindles with every copay. As I ingest it with every antibiotic and painkiller.

I make the Isla Azul paper again. This time my dad doesn't frame it. The article goes out as a warning to everyone in the area to stay vigilant, to be careful, and to not do the dumb things I did. They're trying to be helpful to others but it's insulting when they're quick to point out that if I'd been in a group or if I'd avoided the sandbar that I wasn't even aware I was swimming near, I probably wouldn't have been bit.

Go ahead and educate others on how to avoid an attack – I'm a *huge* advocate for that – but maybe don't print my picture next to it like I'm the author of the *Complete Idiot's Guide on How to be Bitten by a Damn Shark.*

Not only does the entire town know about the attack, they also know Lawson Daniel saved my life. Twice. That's in the paper too, along with a not so subtle insinuation that we're dating.

The same night the article comes out, my phone beeps with a new message from an unknown number.

did you know we're dating?

I glare at my phone, stunned and confused. *Lawson?*

most people call me Law, you know that right?

How did you get my number?

wyatt. you applied for a job at the FF. it was on your resume.

"I hate living in a small town," I grumble.

Dad looks over at me from where he's lying on the couch watching TV. "What'd you say?"

"Nothing. Never mind."

"Who's texting you?"

"Katy."

He snorts, turning back to the TV. "Try again. Katy is at the movies."

"How do you know that?"

"We're buddies online. I saw her post it twenty minutes ago."

"Unreal."

"I told her to bring me back popcorn."

"You get mad at the microwave and yet you're socially networking?"

He shakes his head in disgust. "That thing. Why have a potato button dedicated entirely to undercooking my potato?"

"It's a conspiracy," I reply absently as my phone beeps again.

"So who is it?" Dad asks.

if you still need a job I know of one.

"It's Lawson," I mutter to my dad.

Are you serious? I text Lawson.

"He's trouble. Please tell me you know that."

completely. its out of town tho.

"Everyone knows that, Dad. I've known that since Kindergarten."

How far out of town?

"Try and remember it when you're about to sleep with him."

malibu

"Ugh," I groan, imagining the hour long drive. Then I frown, glancing at my dad. "Wait, what did you say?"

you interested?

I look down at Lawson's message, my frown deepening. "Dad, what did you say?"

"It doesn't matter," he replies, flipping through channels. "A person's got to make their own mistakes in life."

"What is that supposed to mean?"

My phone beeps.

rachel?

Dad sighs as he turns off the TV and hoists himself off the couch. "It means you better answer him. That boy is relentless."

you with me?

I watch my dad leave the room, heading for the kitchen, probably toward a cold beer, and I let my phone sit heavy and silent in my hand. Malibu is a long drive. It's a lot of miles, a lot of gas. It will be a lot of pain. By the end of the summer will it be worth it? Will it have been enough to get me back on track?

I'll never know unless I try.

Yeah, I finally text back, a sinking feeling in my stomach, *I'm with you, Lawson.*

***

Katy goes with me a week later when I drive to Santa Barbara to get my stiches removed. I insist on driving, and even though my leg is aching when we get there twenty minutes later, I'm proud of myself. I've been off my crutches all week, pushing myself to the edge trying to get back to normal. Back to fighting form where I can live my life, get a job, and pretend this all never happened to me. Not the attack, not the injury, and definitely not Lawson Daniel.

"He got you a job in a surf shop in Malibu," Katy reminds me, sitting on a spinning stool at my feet and rotating back and forth. "One he goes to *all* the time. It's gonna be hard to pretend he doesn't exist when you see him every other day."

I purse my lips in annoyance. "I know. He's a hard one to ignore."

"Well, he's Lawson," she says, as though she's reminding me he's some mythical creature. Like a unicorn or a leprechaun. A different species all together, enchanted and strange.

Sad thing is she's not wrong.

He got me the interview at Ambrose Surf within an hour of telling me about it. He even offered to drive me down and go in with me. I told him thanks, but no thanks and that was the end of that conversation. Katy drove me instead. It didn't matter, though. The second I walked in and told them my name, I was ushered to the back with the manager who called me 'Law's friend', never referring me to me by my actual name. I had the job before I even showed up, and even though that bothered me I wasn't in any position to be choosy. Indignant, sure, but not choosy. When they asked me if I could start the next week, I said I could start that day if they wanted me to.

I texted Lawson to thank him, but I didn't get a reply.

"How are you going to get down there four days a week?" Katy asks. "I have day shift at the grocery store. I can't drive you."

"I know. I'll drive myself."

"An hour each way?"

"Yeah."

"You can't do that."

I laugh, scooting back on the long exam table to give my leg some relief, the paper crinkling loudly under my hands. "Why not?"

"Because you barely got us here and it's not even half that distance. You're still in a lot of pain, Rach. You keep trying to act like you're not, but you totally are."

"I'm fine," I tell her lightly, waving away her concerns.

"Yeah, that right there," she says seriously, not dissuaded by my indifference. "That's exactly what I'm talking about."

The door to the exam room opens, letting in a familiar face. Dr. Shinn was there when I was brought into the hospital. He was called in to perform my surgery. To make sure my artery was fully closed and I didn't bleed out in the night from a slow leak.

He's tall and wire thin, of Asian descent with short black hair and almond eyes that show wrinkles at the edges when he smiles. So basically never.

"Rachel," he greets me with a curt nod. His eyes fall on Katy for a brief second before he ignores her entirely. "How are you feeling?"

"Great," I answer quickly.

Katy glares at me.

"No fever symptoms? Inflammation? Swelling? Tenderness?"

"Nope."

"Yes," Katy argues.

"I'm sorry?" Dr. Shinn asks her. He looks down his nose at her, not because he's an asshole but because he's that tall. He looks down at pretty much everyone.

Katy glances quickly between him and I. No one is exactly looking at her warmly. "She's still in pain when she walks," she tells Dr. Shinn, her voice quiet but resolved. "She has tenderness."

"Some amount of discomfort is to be expected. She's still healing."

I swat Katy on the shoulder. "See? It's normal."

Katy ignores me. "She bumped it on a chair back yesterday and couldn't breathe for three seconds."

"Jesus, are you counting my breaths?" I demand.

"No, I'm counting the seconds when you *don't* breathe," she replies hotly. "Like when you went under, I was counting and I was freaking out because I was sure you were never coming back up again and I would be counting for the rest of my life."

"Katy," I say weakly. "I made it. I'm okay."

Dr. Shinn sighs. "Let's try again. Any signs of infection? Tenderness?"

Katy looks at me hard, her mouth tight at the corners.

"Yes," I reply reluctantly.

"Fever?"

"No. I mean, I'm always hot but who isn't? This summer is a killer."

"Are you hot now?'

"Yeah."

"Have you been taking your temperature?"

"No."

He reaches into a cupboard behind him and pulls out a thermometer. He slips a plastic cover over it, then gestures for me to open up so he can put it under my tongue.

We're all oddly silent as we wait. Dr. Shinn touches my forehead at one point, frowning at the feel of my sweat slicked skin. When the time is up he pulls the thermometer out, reads it without reaction, and promptly scribbles a series of notes on my chart.

When he's done writing he looks at me seriously. "You're running a mild fever. Your skin is clammy. I'm going to remove the bandages and take a look at the incision but I'm fairly certain that from what you're both telling me that you have an infection."

"What will that mean?"

He pulls on a pair of gloves. "If the infection was severe you'd know it. Your fever would be through the roof, you'd be faint, and you'd be able to smell it through the bandage. Have you noticed an odd smell?"

"No."

"Good." He cuts the tape holding my bandages in place and methodically begins to unroll them. "Let's see what you have going on."

It's red and puffy, the stitches nearly engulfed in my skin. Dr. Shinn breaks his veneer when he sees it, clicking his tongue and shaking his head slightly.

"Have you been taking your antibiotics?" he asks me when he finishes his examination.

"Yeah, of course. Exactly as it says to on the bottle."

"I'll write you a prescription for something stronger. If that doesn't help we might need to reopen the wounds. There could be more debris inside."

"*More* debris?" Katy asks, her eyes wide. "What was in there to start with?"

"Shark's mouths are filthy places. A bite can transfer sand, shell, gore."

"Gore?"

"It's nothing we can't manage, but we need to be careful until the infection is gone. I wish I hadn't had to put stitches in the wounds. It opened you up further to infection, but several of the bite wounds were too large to heal on their own. They'd never granulate." He clicks his pen sharply, pulling out a prescription pad. "Get this filled immediately. I'm going to send in a nurse with a shot of a strong antibiotic to get you going now and I want you to continue taking this prescription until they're gone completely. We'll reschedule an exam for a week from today."

"What about the stitches?"

"I'm going to remove them now. With the irritation on the skin it's going to hurt."

"Fun," I say drolly.

"I can prescribe you more Percocet if you're afraid of the pain."

"I'm not afraid."

"Good. Afterward you need to take it easy. The wounds aren't totally healed but the sutures have brought them close enough to finish the process on their own. Be careful, rest, stay off that leg. You don't want to reopen them and undo all of the healing you've managed to do. Keep your thigh covered in clean bandages. Give your body time to right itself."

"Isn't that what the drugs are for?" I ask glumly.

"No." He rips the top slip off the pad and hands it to me. "That's what you're for. Be good to your body and it will be good to you. Push it past its limits and it will shit all over you."

My jaw goes slack in surprise as he swears.

I almost pass out when he smiles.

CHAPTER SEVEN

I think about texting Lawson. It seems like the easy way out of what I've gotta say but he's ignored me the last two times I sent him a message and I have no idea what that means, but I know it bugs me. Maybe that's the point. Maybe it's one of his things that he does with women. Gives radio silence to make you come to him.

If it's a tactic, it totally works. I'm at the beach the same day I get my stitches out, waiting in the parking lot next to his car, and as I stand there watching him walk out of the sea at sunset like a god descending to the earth, I think Lawson Daniel is smarter than anyone gives him credit for.

When he sees me he stops, a slow smile forming on his lips. He nods his head toward the beach where his boys are drinking beer and starting a fire. Wyatt and Xavier. Baker with a brunette from the hair salon at the end of the strip.

The sight gives me so much déjà vu that it starts me shivering, my head shaking with the convulsions.

Unfazed, Lawson carries his board up the beach to the parking lot.

"You sure you don't want a beer?" he asks, still smiling. "We're about to roast some brats."

"No, I'm not hungry. Thanks."

He chuckles, lifting his board onto the roof of his car. "You don't learn, do you?"

"Learn what?"

"Or maybe your memory is just shit."

"What are you talking about?" I ask, getting impatient.

He finishes with his board and comes to stand next to me, his hand on the car beside my shoulder. His eyes boring down deep into mine. "I told you not to thank me again."

"Yeah, for saving my life," I scoff. "Wait, is that why you didn't answer my texts? Because I thanked you for the job?"

"Twice."

"Oh my God, I'm so sorry," I say sarcastically. "What a bitch. I thanked you for being nice."

"You shouldn't have to thank a person for being decent."

I smirk up at him. "What if that person is indecent? Shouldn't you thank them for acting outside the norm?"

He laughs, running his free hand over his short hair. "Yeah, you've got a point."

"Don't ignore my texts."

"You gonna keep sending them?"

"I was going to send you one tonight but I figured you weren't going to answer."

He lets his arm go slack, slipping closer until his weight is resting on his elbow and his body is so close to mine his swim trunks are dripping cold salt water on my feet. "What was your text going to say?" he asks, his voice lower than before.

I smile, sidestepping away from him. But I've forgotten myself and I wince as my weight shifts. As my leg catches fire.

His brow creases in concern. "What's wrong? Your leg still?"

"Yeah," I mutter, smoothing my hand gently over my thigh as it throbs. "I had the stitches out today. Turns out I have an infection."

"How bad?"

"It's not bad, I'm fine."

"Did they put you back on antibiotics?"

"Yeah. Stronger ones this time."

"Did they flush the wound again? Was there something stuck inside?"

My hand freezes on my leg as I frown up at him. "How do you know all this stuff?"

He gestures to his own leg. "The coral, remember?"

"You had an infection too? Was some stuck inside?"

"It's pretty common. The ocean isn't a great place to get hurt. She's a dirty girl." He opens his passenger door, gesturing for me to get inside. "Sit down. You shouldn't be standing on it."

I don't fight him because he's right. Because just four hours ago a very stern man was very clear with me about taking it easy and I need to heed that advice, no matter how much I hate it.

I sit down inside Lawson's car, getting all of my appendages inside and feeling crazy weird when he closes the door for me like a gentleman. He goes around the back of the car, messes around in the trunk, and finally climbs inside behind the wheel.

"Here," he hands me a bottled water, dripping wet and freezing cold, "you look like you could use this."

"Thanks."

He pauses with his own drink a moment from his lips. His eyes are on me, hard and impatient.

"Seriously?" I laugh. "I can't thank you for anything?"

"No."

"Why not?"

He smiles before taking a drink. "In the hospital it was because I have a problem with being thanked for things like that."

"Save lives a lot, do you?"

"But now I'm giving you crap about it because it's fun."

"For you, maybe."

He chuckles as he reaches into the backseat. The movement brings him over the center consul and into my space. His chest brushes against my shoulder and I take a sip of my water to appear casual when what I really am is twitchy.

Lawson sits back in his seat before yanking a T-shirt over his head and pulling it down his torso. The shade is familiar and it takes me a second to realize the logo on the front is the same one painted on the window at Ambrose Surf.

"So," he begins, "what was the text going to say?"

I point to his shirt. "That I can't work there after all. My doctor wants me to take it easy and rest so I need to keep trying to find something here in town. I can't drive an hour and back to work."

"Your doctor said you could work but not drive?"

"Not exactly."

"What exactly did he say?"

"I told you. He wants me to rest."

"And you think 'rest' means work?"

I set my drink down in the cup holder hard, the cold water sloshing dangerously close to the open top.

He holds up his hand. "Before you go off on me, can I tell you something?"

"What?"

"You're hot."

I sigh. "Are you kidding me, dude? Are you ever not *on*?"

"I'm not hitting on you," he promises with a grin. "I'm telling you that that's why they hired you at Ambrose. It's a sausage fest down there. They were looking for a hot beach girl to spice things up. Pull in the high school guys. I told them I knew a beautiful girl with basic knowledge about boards who could count correct change. The second they saw you, you had the job."

"That is...not that much worse than how I thought I got the job anyway," I reply unhappily.

"You didn't blow Don, did you? 'Cause you did not need to do that."

"You're gross."

"I'm not. A blowjob is a beautiful thing."

"Yeah, if you're not the one with a nose full of ball hair."

"You're blowing some unkempt bros."

"I'm not blowing anybody," I groan. "Least of

all the bald old guy with the ugly Hawaiian shirt in the back of a surf shop."

"You could do worse."

I ignore that entirely. "It doesn't matter why they hired me. I can't stand there at the register for an entire shift."

"Wear V-necks. They'll let you sit on a stool and the guys can look down your shirt."

"Even if I were okay with that, I can't make the drive. It's too long."

"How many days a week?"

"Four."

"I'll drive you."

I stare straight ahead at the darkening horizon, my heart slowly rising in my throat. The blue-black water rolls toward the shore with glowing white tips that form and fade so slowly it's like sleeping. It's like a dream you can't get your head around before it's gone and you're on to the next. It's a dream I thought I understood.

Then one day I woke up and it turned out to be a nightmare.

"Rachel?"

I jerk my head around to look at him. He's concerned again, his eyes electric and strange in the low light. "Yeah?"

"You spaced out there for a second."

"Sorry," I laugh nervously. "I'm tired. Long day."

He reaches out and starts the engine. "Buckle up."

"What? No. Where are we going?"

"To your house." He pulls his seatbelt into

place, snapping it securely. "I'm driving you home."

"Lawson, no, you can't. My car is here."

"Give me your keys. I'll get one of the guys to help me drive it back to your place later."

"I can drive."

"You shouldn't have been doing it before and I'm sure you're not supposed to be doing it now."

"It doesn't mean I can't," I protest, bristling as he puts the car in reverse. I reach for the door but he's already moving. "Stop, seriously."

"Buckle up, seriously."

"Stop the car."

"No."

"Lawson Daniel," I snap, irritated.

He grins. "I know you're mad but I'm not watching you hobble across this lot to your car and drive home in pain."

"Everyone needs to calm down. It's not that big of a deal."

He slams on the brakes. The car jolts, throwing me toward the dash. I brace myself with my hands and my feet, crying out in uncontrollably when a band of pain wraps around my thigh and clenches it tightly.

"You asshole," I gasp, my throat closing tightly against the pain.

"How big of a deal is it now?" he asks dispassionately.

I turn my head to glare at him, stunned by his empty tone. When I see his face it's even worse. It's blank, all concern gone. "What is your problem?"

"Quit acting like it didn't happen," he tells me

firmly. "Quit acting like it's no big deal. You could have died, Rachel. You could have drowned, you could have been eaten, you could have lost your entire fucking leg in the mouth of a shark."

"Shut up!" I shout, the words exploding out of me in a roll of rage I didn't know I had in me.

Lawson isn't impressed by it. "It's okay to be hurt and it's okay to be scared, but you gotta get over it. You're hurt in your head as much as you are in your leg and you can't just act like it's not happening and expect it to go away."

"What do you want me to do? Cry about it?"

"Have you? Since it happened, have you cried?"

"No."

"That's messed up."

"Who are you to tell me how to feel?"

That gets him.

He hesitates, his eyes on mine but his thoughts are a million miles away. A million minutes to another time and another moment that I don't understand because I can't see it. Not the way he does.

"You're right," he eventually answers quietly. "It's not my business. But let me drive you home tonight at least."

"Why?"

"Because I want to."

That's all the answer he gives me and as it turns out it's all the answer I need. If he'd said it was because I'm hurt and that I can't drive myself, I would be out of that car so fast his head would swim. But he makes it so it's not about me. He's not doing me a favor so I don't have to thank him – not that he'd let me anyway – but it saves my pride. That's something I'm starting to realize is important to me. Something I'm pretty sure Lawson already knew.

And for the second time that day it occurs to me that Lawson Daniel is more clever than anyone suspects.

I sit back, buckle my seatbelt, and even though we don't speak on the drive home, he convinces me to take him up on his offer. I agree to let him drive me to Malibu.

CHAPTER EIGHT

Two days later and Lawson is in my driveway again. It's becoming a habit. A thing. A thing that doesn't feel insane anymore and that's what's so damn freaky about it.

"I feel bad about this," I tell him, lowering myself carefully into Lawson's car.

He doesn't help me but he waits until I'm inside before getting into his seat behind the wheel. When he turns on the engine cold air blasts blissfully from the vents, making me sigh in relief.

My fever is gone but this summer is a scorcher. We're only a week away from July and the temperatures are already kissing the underside of one hundred during the day and dropping down to the seventies at night if we're lucky. It's cooler down by the water and I hear from Katy that parties have been going on just about every night. I also hear that Lawson is always there and that he rarely goes home alone.

"It's no problem. I'm down there all the time anyway," he promises me. "The surfing in Malibu is insane."

"Better than Isla Azul?"

"Everything is better than Isla Azul," he mumbles, backing out of my driveway and quickly pulling us away from my neighborhood.

I'm grateful my dad is at work at the body shop. He wouldn't be happy to see me in a car with Lawson, though I'm sure he'll hear about it through the grapevine before we even make it out of town.

I wonder, in the version he hears will I be wearing any underwear?

I point to the roof of the car where I saw a surfboard strapped to the top. "What's her name?"

Lawson grins. "Didn't I introduce you the other night?"

"No. Super rude of you."

"Christa."

I wrinkle my nose. "Christa?"

"What's wrong with Christa?"

"I don't know. I think I prefer Layla, though."

"Yeah," he agrees heavily. "Me too."

I sneak a glance at him. His tone is almost sad but his face is perfectly calm. At ease.

"Why don't you still use her?" I ask.

He smiles, leaning his body to the left against the door and expertly driving us down the coast with one hand. "Aren't you the one who gave me a hard time for surfing at all after what happened? Now you want me to use the same board I brought you to shore on?"

"Like you care what I think," I laugh. "You're still surfing. Why not use the board you love?"

"I told you. She's retired."

"Because of me?"

"Yeah."

I blink, staggered by the honesty of his answer. "I wouldn't care if you used it. The idea doesn't bother me."

"Of course it doesn't," he jabs under his breath.

"What?"

He looks at me briefly, appraising my expression, and decides to shift the gears on the conversation. "Look, it's not a big deal. That board..." he laughs to himself, shifting his hand on the steering wheel. "You're gonna make fun of me for this."

"For what?"

"That board has a weird vibe now."

"I jinxed your board?"

"Not you. Not specifically. More like that day."

"Does it have bad juju? Can you get a gypsy woman to lift the curse?"

He shakes his head. "I knew you'd make fun of it."

"You're being serious?"

"I was, yeah."

"Sorry," I apologize, trying to sound contrite.

The truth is that I *do* get it. I understand that almost all athletes are at least a little bit superstitious, so it doesn't exactly shock me that Lawson hung up the board I bled on. What's throwing me for a loop is the 'vibe' comment. It's a little earthy, a little too spiritual of a term for a guy I've always seen as nothing but a beer swigging, pot smoking, sex fiend. I'm still getting used to Lawson being a human being. He's been a caricature to me for so long – a hot guy with a cocky grin, a board under his feet, beer in his hand, and a joint between his lips – that it's hard to wrap my head around him being... I don't know. Real, I guess.

"It's alright. Christa's a good board," he says with a shrug. "She's solid. I'll stick with her until I find another one like Layla."

"Does the board make that big of a difference? I mean, you're crazy talented. I would think you could surf any board any time."

He looks at me sideways, his brows raised skeptically. "Can you play any piano any time, to perfection?"

"Yes."

He laughs at my bold answer, the sound rough and rumbling in the small interior of the car. It swirls around me, coming in close. Pressing against me, edging out the cold air and warming my skin.

"Alright, yeah, 'cause you're good," he says, still chuckling. "But would you enjoy it? Can you love the music you're making out of any piano anyone puts in front of you, or does it matter? If you were told the keys were real ivory and an animal was killed to make them, would you feel good about pressing them?"

I sigh, relenting. "Yeah, you're right. It would make a difference. I wouldn't want to touch that piano. I definitely wouldn't want to make music on it."

"And if you're not loving it, then why do it?"

"I'm surprised you knew I play piano."

He scoffs. "Come on, Rach, give me some credit. We've gone to school together since we were five. I know you play the piano. Shit, you played at graduation!"

"You remember that?" I ask doubtfully.

"It was only three years ago."

"Yeah, but I assumed you were baked out of your mind at the time."

He smiles, his throat constricting with a silent chuckle. "Unless Kermit the Frog really was our valedictorian, yeah. I was baked. But I remember you playing and I remember it being beautiful."

"What'd I play?"

He briefly meets my eyes and my challenge head on. No hesitation. No doubts.

"*Today*," he answers confidently. "Smashing Pumpkins. Fucking. Beautiful."

I smile. "I can't believe you remember that."

"Why not? You remembered that I was baked."

"You were always baked."

"And you were always being beautiful," he replies quietly. Earnestly.

It's the second time he's called me beautiful in as many days and, yeah, I'm counting. I'm trying to watch my back here. I'm in dangerous waters. Murky, uncharted waters, and I'm trying to see the sandbar this time before it's too late.

***

They give me a stool along with a tank top a size too small for me that says 'Ambrose Surf' across the front. It rides up to nearly my belly button and I'd tug it down to cover my midriff if that didn't mean the top would pop right off my breasts. But I let it go because whatever. Seriously, that's where I'm at with the whole job thing. With this summer in general. Whatever. I need the money and if I was a bartender or a waitress at one of these clubs here in Malibu, they'd be asking me to wear the same. Probably worse.

The assistant manager, Marvin, sets me up at the register. He asks me if I've ever used a cash register before, I say I have, and he walks away. That's my training. It's a pretty laid back place and I notice right away that what it really is more than a store is a hang out. There are times all throughout the day that Marvin and the owner, Don, spend over an hour shooting the shit with customers about pretty much everything under the sun and in the surf. They swap stories, talk waves, and when a regular comes in for no other discernible reason than to say 'what's up', they're greeted at the door like Norm walking into Cheers.

"Law!"

He walks in slowly, one hand in the pocket of his cargo shorts, the other waving to the room of seven or so guys greeting him.

"'Sup," he says in return, his voice deep and subdued. He moves slowly across the room, lazily, as though he's still in the water. Like he's floating and drifting with the tide.

I watch him and I wonder if his mellow is from a day in the curl or if he's had some kind of herbal refreshment.

"You guys been good to my girl?" he asks, nodding toward me at the register.

"Not your girl," I clarify to the room.

"Not yet."

I laugh, standing slowly to avoid having to look him in the face. I don't want him to see me blush at his words.

He comes over to the counter and leans against it. With me standing it puts him eye level with my boobs. "You want to give it a try yet?" he asks me, his voice hushed.

"Try what?" I mock whisper.

"Saying my name. Feeling that rush."

"I've said your name recently. I think the last time I did it I felt angry."

"That's the problem. You only say it when you're mad at me. Try it now."

"Who says I'm not mad at you now?"

He smiles up at me, his eyes dancing green waters. "What's the matter, Rachel? Are you scared you'll like it?"

"Did that do it for you just then? Saying my name?"

He lays his bare arm out on counter, never breaking eye contact. "It gave me goosebumps."

I chuckle, looking down at his tan skin covered in sun-bleached hairs. Hairs that are standing on end.

My smile fades, my eyes jumping back to his. He's waiting for me.

"I wouldn't lie to you," he mumbles. "I meant it. Every time I say your name I get chills."

I swallow hard. "That's not normal."

"No, it's not." He stands up slowly, a smile building on his lips as he backs away. "But I like it. Rachel."

He's too far away to tell if it happens again, but I know it does. I know he feels that shiver, that thrill, and the freaky part isn't that it happens. It's that I *hope* it happened.

These waters are not only murky.
They're black as midnight.

CHAPTER NINE

When my shift is over Lawson is still there in the store. It's been almost two hours but he hangs out in the corner with the guys, a group that grows and thins every twenty minutes or so, but it's always there in some shape or form. But when Lawson is there, he's the center of it. He's the one with the stories they all ask to hear, the one people introduce their friends to. He's the one who draws in a crowd and I smile as I watch him, thinking he's better for business than I would be sitting here completely naked. People love him whether they know him or not because he's a legend. He's a king in their community, and as I watch people circle around him I wonder what that's like. I wonder if this gives him goosebumps too.

"You ready to go?" he asks me when my shift is over.

I nod, grabbing my T-shirt I was wearing when I came in and following him to the door. He holds it open for me, waving goodbye to his fan club when he follows me outside. I make sure I'm out of view of the store windows before I pull my shirt on over the tank top, covering myself up.

Lawson laughs at me. "It's not that bad."

"No, it's not," I concede. "But my dad

wouldn't like it and he has friends down here. If it got back to him that I was walking down the street with the girls busting out I'd never hear the end of it."

"Would it be worse than if he found out I drove you?"

"Probably not, but I'm sure that's circulated the town already."

He nods heavily. "Probably before we made it out of your driveway."

"I love Isla Azul, but I hate that about it," I say sourly.

"The gossip?"

"Yeah. Everybody knows everybody's business."

"And if you manage to keep a secret, everybody knows you have a secret."

"And they guess at it, making up stories that are bigger than the actual secret."

When we get to the car he opens my door for me, actually taking hold of my elbow gently and helping me lower myself into the car. His face is vacant, his eyes far away, and I don't think he realizes he's doing it. He's running on auto-pilot and apparently that pilot is a tad chivalrous. I'm sure he'll still sip whiskey in the cockpit and feel up a stewardess by the bathrooms, but he'll be sweet about it. He'll make her feel like a lady.

"I wanna take you somewhere," he tells me abruptly.

I pause with my seatbelt in my hands, looking up at him as he leans in between the open door and the car. "Where? Here in Malibu?"

LAWLESS

"No. In Isla Azul."

"Where?"

"It's a surprise."

"I don't know if you'll understand this or not," I warn him slowly, "but lately I'm not a big fan of surprises."

He smiles. "It's a good surprise. It'll get the gossips going."

"I don't want you to get me pregnant."

"What?" he chuckles.

"Sure it'd be good for a laugh, shake the town up and shame my family, but then I'm strapped with a baby. Your baby, and that's just unnerving."

"I'm not going to get you pregnant," he swears. "I'm not even going to kiss you."

I look out the windshield, debating. It'll be dark by the time we get home. He knows that. I've lived my entire life in that town – what could he possibly hope to surprise me with? And how am I going to see it in the dark?

In the end it's that, the curiosity, that gets me.

"Alright, yeah," I tell him with a shrug. "Let's do it."

"You'll probably regret this."

I laugh. "You're supposed to tell me I *won't* regret it."

"I know," he says seriously, "but I don't want to lie to you."

An hour later the sun has set, we've made it to Isla Azul, and I know exactly where we're going.

"This is a make out spot," I tell him accusingly.

He parks us on the bluff overlooking the ocean where it drifts off to infinity as it merges with the night sky. We're far from the lights of any town on the coast and the stars are out in full force as a cool breeze blows in through the open windows. He's even opened the sunroof so I can see up above us where the moon hangs happy and heavy in the sky.

"For some people, yeah, it's a make out spot," he acknowledges.

"For you for sure. I've heard stories from the whore's mouth a few times about you and—"

"Whoa, whoa," he laughs, holding up his hands in a T symbol. "Time out. What'd you say? You heard stories from where?"

"The horse's mouth."

"That's not what you said."

"What'd I say?"

His shoulders shake with laughter as he lets his head fall back against the seat. "You said 'whore's mouth'."

I slap his arm hard. "No, I didn't!"

"Yes, you did! Clear as day."

I look out the windshield at the darkness, trying to remember. "Oh God, did I?"

"Yep."

"Well, that's telling."

"You think any girl that hooks up with me is a whore."

"That's not true."

He rolls his head toward me, his eyes narrowed skeptically. "Come on."

"Alright, yes," I relent. "Maybe I do."

"That's kind of bitchy."

"Did you just call me a bitch?"

"No, I said it's kind of bitchy to assume all of

74

my girlfriends are whores."

I quirk my eyebrow at him dubiously. "Really?"

He smiles and shrugs. "Okay, maybe not girlfriends. More like…"

"Conquests?"

"No, that's not what it's about."

"What's it about then?"

"Being alone."

I freeze, unsure what to do with that. It's so boldly honest, so blatantly raw that it stuns me. I wasn't expecting it and now that it's out there and I'm ignoring it I feel like I'm blowing it. Like there should be some perfect response to that statement that will get him talking, get him to open up further and then… what? I'll make it all better? I'll fix him? We'll be there for each other so the world isn't so lonely because, hey, guess what?

I'm alone too.

"Interim intimates," I tell him with a smile I don't feel.

He chuckles with amusement he doesn't mean. "Perfect."

"And no, I don't really think they're all whores."

"But you think I am."

"You've slept around a lot," I remind him.

"How many people have you slept with?"

Three.

"No way," I chuckle. "I'm not playing this game."

"It's not a game."

"Are you sure? Because it's so much fun."

"How many?"

"How many have *you* slept with?"

"Eight," he answers instantly, his face so serious it's almost too much.

I eye him uncertainly. "They say a guy will always double his number but with you I'm inclined to think you'd cut it in half."

He smiles. "It's eight. No math required."

"Good God, I think I actually believe you," I sigh sadly.

"What?" he asks defensively. "Eight's not that bad."

"No, it's not. That's not what's bothering me."

"It bothers you that you trust me?"

"A little bit."

He winces. "Ouch."

"Three."

Now I have his attention. He sits up and turns toward me. "You've slept with three guys?"

"Yes."

"Anyone I know?"

Yes.

"No."

"You're lying."

"You probably are too."

He grins slyly, the light from the dashboard casting shadows over his face, painting him a villain.

"Maybe."

"How many?" I insist.

"Nine."

"Baker."

His eyes go wide, his mouth dropping open.

"Baker Baker? My boy Baker?"

I smile faintly. "Well, at the time he was more *my boy* Baker."

He grins, offering me his knuckles. "Respect."

"No."

"Come on," he pleads, shaking his fist eagerly.

I sigh before bumping it.

"Nice," he says, sitting back in his seat happily. "I can't believe Baker never told me."

"Remind me to thank him for that."

"You shouldn't have to."

"You don't get to police all of my niceties, Law."

He rolls his head toward me. "Cheater."

"At what?"

"You shortened it. Say it, the whole thing."

I shake my head, looking away. "Are you still on this?"

"I will be until you try."

"That'll be fun for me."

"You won't because you're scared you'll like it." He crosses his arms over his chest, settling in and closing his eyes. "I think you're scared of a lot of things."

"You're wrong."

"Okay."

"*Lawson*," I pronounce emphatically. "There. I said it and I didn't feel anything."

"You didn't say it right."

I groan, letting my head fall back and closing my eyes as well. I listen to the sound of the ocean outside the windows. The rush of the wind. It's like breathing. In and out. Slow and steady. It falls in time with the rhythm of Lawson's breath, taking mine with it until the interior of the car and the exterior of the world are in sync. Until I can't tell where it ends and I begin. I feel myself drifting away on the water, in the dark. I should be afraid but I'm not. I can feel him there with me. I can hear him and smell him and if I wanted to I know I could touch him. And I do – I want to. I want to hold his hand the way I did when he pulled me up. But I don't because it won't be the same this time.

This time Lawson Daniel can't save me.

This time he'll ruin me.

***

"Rachel."

I frown, blinking roughly trying to clear my sight but no matter how many times I do it I still can't see a thing. For a second I panic, not sure where I am, but then I remember. The bluff. The car.

Lawson's car.

I open my eyes wide, taking in the darkness. His dashboard is blank, just a faint outline of black on black. The sea continues to roar outside because it never stops, not for anyone or anything, and the few cars that were with us before are gone now. We're alone. Just me and Lawson Daniel hovering somewhere between the big, wide ocean and the endless sky above us.

It's disorienting. I'm still waking up, still half asleep, caught halfway between heaven and earth, and when his lips touch mine I'm somewhere else entirely. I'm in the air and under the water. I'm drowning and I'm flying.

His hand cups my face, warm and calloused the way I remember it. The way I want it to be. It's what I need, *he's* what I need, and I open like a lock dying to be sprung, my lips parting and welcoming his tongue with mine. His hand slips back into my hair, holding me more firmly to him, and I whimper somewhere in the back of my throat. A small needy sound that sends his breathing ragged and brings him closer to me. He's nearly on top of me and I want him there. I want him pressing down on me. I want his hands. I want his breath, his lips, his scent, his eyes.

I want *him*.

And he knows it because Lawson Daniel always knows.

He reaches around and pulls a lever that lowers my seatback. He guides it down slowly until I'm lying on my back, but then he's gone. He's over the center console, into the back seat, and he's pulling me with him. He's helping me climb and fumble back with him until he's laying down and I'm straddling his waist and my shirt is disappearing along with his shorts. Then mine. Then his shirt. My bra. His boxers.

It happens so fast, like magic or lightning. One minute I'm asleep the next I'm in nothing but my underwear looking down into those perfect green of his eyes as he rolls on a condom, and I'm wondering how I got here. I'm wondering how long I can stay.

Lawson touches me slowly. He caresses every

piece of exposed skin he can find, searching for more until I'm naked and shivering, writhing against him, and he's groaning in this tortured way that makes me feel alive and beautiful. Powerful. I run my fingertips slowly across his skin, gently as though I'm feeling out a new piano, and I feel it pebble with chills and excitement. With the rush.

And I want it. I want it more than my next breath. I want it more than I want sex, more than I want him. More than I want to leave this town and so much more than I want to stay. I want to feel that excitement, to feel like I crave and fear something so much that my body reacts to it in a primal way.

He looks up at me with hooded eyes full of everything I'm feeling and his hands are on my hips and I'm hunching down as I rise up, hovering above him. I slip down slowly, letting him in. All of him. Every inch, every ounce, every breath he breathes and shuddering gasp he makes is mine inside my chest. I echo it and I feel my entire body come alive like fire as I move against him.

"Rachel," he grunts, his voice breaking on my name and crumbling like stardust across his skin where I can feel it under my fingers mixed with his sweat and the sea salt air. "I want to hear you say it. I want to see you feel it."

I smile faintly, smoothing my palms over his chest and leaning my body down against his. My leg burns with the movement but I don't care. I get as close to him as I can, take him in as deep as my body will allow as I press my lips against his ear, and I whisper his name once.

"Lawson."

I say it right this time. I know because I feel it everywhere. I feel my skin prickle with excitement. My stomach knots with an anxious energy, and when he wraps his arms around me to hold me to him tightly, his teeth sinking gently into my shoulder with a tender bite, I feel my body detonate in a showering explosion of life and lust and fear that makes me cry out tremulously.

Lawson growls deep in his chest, a rumbling I feel through my breasts and my body as he rocks it back and forth over his hips, and then he's clinging to me. His hands are in my hair pulling hard and his breathing is erratic and desperate.

When he stills I move to roll off him, but he holds me in place, pinning my body to his. I lift my head to look down at him and he moves his hands to push my wild hair aside, unburying my eyes. When he finds them he kisses me softly on the lips.

"Stay," he whispers roughly, his face tired and happy.

"I should go home," I tell him, not knowing exactly why. It's not what I want.

Thank God Lawson knows that.

He nods solemnly, running the pad of his thumb over my cheek. "I know. And I'll get you there. But for now I'm asking you to stay with me."

I lower my cheek to his chest and settle in against his body. "Okay," I tell him quietly. Contentedly. "I'll stay with you. I promise."

It's word for word what he told me on the beach after he saved my life. I don't know why I say it the way I do. I don't know what exactly I've just promised him or if he even wanted me to, but as

I say it I know it's the truth because there's something here that I need. That I crave. That I'd kill for. That I've been dying for.

And it's not the sex. It's the man. Not the myth or the legend or the rumors. It's him.

It's Lawson.

CHAPTER TEN

The next morning my ass is dragging. I'm exhausted. I feel like I'm hung over, and as I'm getting ready for work at the crack of dawn I'm trying really hard not to think about why. To not relive it over and over again in my mind, my body clenching low and tight at the memory.

Lawson's chest.

Lawson's hands.

Lawson's moans.

Lawson's di—

"You came in late."

I spin around with my heart in my throat. Dad is there in the doorway to the kitchen, watching me stare into nothing by the sink. An empty coffee cup dangles from my hand, an equally empty coffee pot sitting cold on the maker's base in front of me. I've been standing here waiting for coffee to brew. Coffee I never made.

I need to get it together.

"Uh, yeah," I mutter, putting the mug down and stepping away from the counter. "Lawson and I hung out for a while after work."

"He drove you?"

I'm so grateful to him for that – for asking what he already knows. What the entire town already knows. He's giving me the chance to lie about it if I want to and even though we'll both know it's a lie, I know he'll let me have it.

"Yeah," I answer honestly. "He surfs down there all the time. He offered to drive me down and back while my leg is healing."

"Could take all summer."

"I know."

"Does he?"

"Yeah."

"Huh," he mutters.

I suppress a sigh. "What?"

Dad shakes his head, grabbing his lunch bag out of the refrigerator and heading for the back door. "Long commitment for Lawson Daniel," he says evenly.

He pulls the door closed hard behind him.

I'm surprised by the relief I feel when Lawson pulls into my driveway ten minutes later. A part of me, small but persuasive, was convinced he would disappear after what happened last night.

An even smaller part kind of wanted him to.

I don't know what to do with this. With what happened. I don't know what it means or if it means anything other than the fact that we're attracted to each other and it felt good. *Really, really* good. I'm no stranger to sex. I've had good, I've had bad, and I've had a lot of in between, but last night was something singular. It was intense and natural as the tide, and I imagine it was just as inevitable.

But was it a one-time thing? Was it a mistake? Are we going to pretend it never happened?

Are we going to do it again?

He doesn't get out of the car when I come outside. He doesn't open my door the way he has before. He doesn't even look up. As I approach the passenger door I can see him through the windshield, his head down over the phone in his hands. He's texting quickly, his fingers flying over the keys.

When I open the door he looks up, a forced smile on his face as he deftly darkens his phone's screen and drops it into a cup holder. "Hey," he greets me warmly, his tone more genuine than his smile.

"Hi."

"How are you feelin'?"

I lower myself slowly into the car and pull the door closed behind me. "Okay. Tired."

"Wild night?"

I shrug. "Pretty boring, actually."

"Really? Nothing fun or exciting?"

"Stayed home. Read a book." I lift my hands and dance my fingers for him to see. "Painted my nails. What about you?"

"Same old, same old."

"You surfed?"

He grins. "Banged a chick."

I laugh, swatting him hard on the arm. He pretends to cringe from it but then he's rushing toward it. He's leaning over the console, he's in my space, and his lips are on mine silencing my laughter and replacing it with something else entirely. Something far more raw and rough. It's not invasive, he doesn't involve his tongue, but it's intimate. He kisses me with feeling, intensity, and I melt into the seat like hot butter even as my skin explodes in goosebumps.

"I thought about you all night," he mumbles against my mouth. "I haven't slept. I haven't showered. I can still smell you on my skin." He licks a line along my lower lip, making me shiver. "I can still feel you."

I feel my body respond to him and his words, but this is not the time and my driveway in broad daylight is absolutely not the place. I put my hands on the sides of his face and move it back, away from mine. I come up for air before he can pull me any farther under.

"I have to go to work," I remind him.

He grins, crooked and boyish and unashamed. "You sure you don't want to blow it off and spend the day with me? Take a cooler down to the water. You in that purple bikini—"

"How do you know the colors of my bikinis? I was wearing a yellow one the night you saved me."

He sits back in his seat, popping the car into gear. "I know because I've seen you in probably ten of them at the beach. I like the purple one."

"I'm scared to ask why."

"It makes your eyes look warmer."

"Ha," I laugh shortly. "Not buying it. Try again."

"It looks good with your blond hair?"

"Nope."

"It makes your ass look tight."

"There it is."

The drive down to Malibu is quiet. Quiet, but not awkward. The silence isn't an avoidance, it simply *is*. It feels easy being here with him. Simple when I thought it'd be complicated. I'm enjoying just being with Lawson, and if I'm not reading him wrong, he's enjoying it too.

He reaches over every now and then and touches my hand. He doesn't take it in his to hold it. He only touches it. Caresses it lightly, a faint smile on his lips as he drives, like he's getting something from it. Something small but saccharine, and it's right and just because it gives something to me in return. It gives me a calm I didn't know I needed. Being with him like this relieves an anxiety in my blood, a tightness in my bones and my heart that turns me to liquid and sets me free. It feels dangerous and wild but I like it too much to care. I'm too comfortable to know how afraid I should be.

"You're off at four?" Lawson asks as he pulls up in front of Ambrose Surf.

"Yeah, four today. I close again tomorrow. Good news is we get to sleep in."

He grins. "I don't sleep in. I'll be up at five to get out in the water by six."

"That's insane," I mutter, shaking my head.

"You've never surfed that early?"

"I've only surfed a handful of times and, no, it was never before noon."

"I'll come get you tomorrow morning. We'll hit the beach before the sun and you'll see what I'm talking about."

I feel my face fall as my stomach drops out. He sees it, he has to, but he doesn't react. He waits, watching me.

"I think I'd rather sleep in."

"You mean you're scared of going in the ocean again."

"Mostly that, yeah," I admit, figuring what's the point in lying?

His eyes tighten at the edges. "You gotta get over that. If you don't do it now it will be harder later."

I rub my hand absently along my thigh. "I'm not ready yet, Lawson. You need to leave this alone."

He looks away, nodding reluctantly. "Alright, fine. I'll drop it for now."

"Forever."

"For now," he chuckles. "But you gotta give me the beach in exchange for my silence."

"Your eternal silence."

"Temporary silence. There's a party tonight. Bonfire, beer, music – the whole deal. And you're going."

I'm already shaking my head. "I told you, I'm tired. I'm going home tonight and going to sleep."

"How are you gonna get there?"

I narrow my eyes at him. "You're driving me."

"Am I?"

"Lawson Daniel."

He laughs, bringing his eyes back to mine. "Am I in trouble?"

"You will be if you don't drive me home tonight."

"I will. After the party."

"I told you—"

"And I'm asking you," he interrupts. "I'm

asking you to try. Not the water, just the beach. Go past the parking lot. Sit by the fire, have a beer, and let it be okay to be there for a few hours. That's all I'm asking."

I sigh, feeling frightened and defeated because I know he's right. I'm a coastal California girl. The Pacific is in my blood. I need it to live, to breathe, and deep down I hate that I'm afraid of it. I feel like I kept my life and my leg that day but I lost something else. I lost my heartbeat, my spirit, and being with Lawson... I don't know exactly what it is about him, but he gives me that missing piece back, if just for a moment. Maybe it's because he *is* the sea. He's the waves and the water. The warm sun on my skin and the soft sand under my feet.

Sand that shifts in the wind and slips away with the tide.

His phone beeps several times, the sound of text messages pouring in. He frowns down at it in the cup holder. He looks annoyed, an expression I can't believe I've never seen on him before. It looks so odd, his strong features looking sharp and angular. Angry.

"I gotta get inside," I tell him, opening my door. "I'll see you later?"

He glances up at me, his eyes distant. "Yeah. Have a good day."

"Thanks. You too."

I look back over my shoulder when I get to the front of the store. His car is still parked there on the street, his head hunched down. His fingers probably working furious over the keys on his phone.

**

I call Katy on my lunch break. She's just about to go to start work herself down at the grocery store and I catch her making a mad dash across the parking lot trying not to be late.

"You're serious?" she asks breathily. "You're going to the party tonight?"

"Apparently, yeah."

"Don't be excited about it or anything."

"I would be if it was my choice."

"How is it not?"

"Lawson is blackmailing me."

"You've gotta be one of the only girls in Isla Azul who has ever told that boy no," she says with admiration.

Not anymore.

I think about telling her. I can't right now because she's going to be late and the fact that I slept with Lawson is more than a quick conversation. It's a Congressional Meeting. A goddam UN Summit. It's definitely not something you drop on someone and run away.

Maybe it's not something you tell anyone at all. Ever.

I still don't know if it's going to happen again. I want it to, I so massively do, and it's obvious Lawson does to, but what will that mean? I have no idea. I'm leaving at the end of the summer and not looking to start a relationship, and let's be real – Lawson Daniel doesn't do relationships. So what is it then? A fling? I could handle a fling. It might be good for me. One last goodbye to Isla Azul. One last kiss from California to get me through the long dark winter in Boston.

"Shit," Katy curses under her breath. "I gotta go. My boss just saw me coming in and she's glaring at me."

I look down at my watch. "You're not late yet are you?"

"No, but that bitch thinks anyone not here ten minutes early is late. I swear, I do not get paid enough to work for this woman."

"You should take this job when I leave. It's cake. You just have to sit there and look pretty."

"I might take it from you now."

"Over my dead body. I need a plane ticket first."

"Good luck with that. I'll talk to you later."

She's gone before I can say goodbye.

CHAPTER ELEVEN

Lawson's phone beeps with messages the entire drive back home. We're nearly there, nearly to the shore, and my nerves are so shot that I can't take it. When it beeps again I have to bite back a scream.

"Are you going to answer that?" I snap.

He casts me a frown, surprised by my vicious tone. "No. I'm not going to text and drive."

"Well can I answer it then because it's driving me crazy?"

"No," he laughs. "I'll turn it on silent if it bothers you that much."

"It doesn't bother me."

"I'd hate to see you bothered, then," he mutters, reaching down and silencing his phone.

I sigh, trying to force myself to calm but it doesn't come. My good leg is twitching. My hands are clasping and unclasping anxiously in my lap, over and over. Luckily I'm on the land side of the car as we head north, Lawson sitting next to the water. The world on my side is all brown earth and yellowed bushes. Thirsty, tired trees leaning away from the road, pushed by the wind all their lives until they're practically growing sideways. They're leaning away from the water, like they know. Like they're just as desperate to avoid it as I am.

"It's Aaron," he tells me quietly.

I choke on my breath, my eyes bugging out of my head as I spin around to look at him. He isn't fazed. He sits there calm as anything, his arm up on the door and his fingers lightly touching his temple as his other hand steers us up the winding coast.

I haven't heard Aaron's name spoken in almost a year. Not from anyone but Katy and she's been trying very hard not to say it anymore. She tries even harder not to think it, but I don't believe she succeeds. I'm pretty sure she thinks about him every single day. I just hope she isn't crying every day anymore.

"How is he?" I tread softly, as though I'm speaking to a beautiful bird that could take flight and disappear forever if I'm not very, very careful.

Lawson coughs, shifting in his seat. "He's okay. He's bugging me."

"About what?"

"Everything. You're lucky you're an only child."

"Not always. It gets lonely." I pause, not sure if it's okay to ask more. I wonder if I'm allowed to say his name too. "Is Aa—"

"I just didn't want you to think it was a girl," Lawson explains in an odd rush. He chuckles, relaxing his features and giving me an easy grin, his entire demeanor changing in an instant. "I'm not a total asshole. I wouldn't do that."

"Do what?"

"Be with you and hit up another girl. That's a dick move, even for me."

I shrug, pretending not to care but in reality I

relax a little inside. "I don't expect anything from you."

He doesn't say anything to that, but the tone in the car shifts perceptibly. The air gets heavier, tighter. More violently strung like a piano wire tuned too hard, but when I sneak a glance in his direction I find his face a mask of utter calm.

I do not, however, bring up his brother again.

When we pull into the parking lot at the beach I'm immediately looking for Katy. I want to run to her, to tell her what Lawson said, but then I really think about it. What will I say?

Lawson talked about Aaron. He's alive! He has a cell phone that he's not calling you with. He's okay. He's annoying.

That's really all I know. Not enough to soothe any open wounds Katy still has. In fact, it's just enough to rip them wide open. To pour sea salt inside that will burn and fester for days, bringing tears to her eyes and sleepless nights to her mind. It's the last thing she needs, so as wrong as it feels to hide it from her, I know I can't tell her anything.

"You okay?" Lawson asks quietly.

I give him a half-hearted smile. "Yeah, just tired."

"You don't really have to do this. Not tonight. If you want me to take you home I will."

I gaze out through the windshield to the group gathering by the fire pit. His boys are there. Wyatt, Xander, Baker, Kinnser. Katy's car is in the parking lot but I don't see her. There are other girls though. Lots of them. All with perfect bodies in perfect bikinis. Body's that are whole and unhurt.

Untattered and unbroken. They're not afraid of the water. They're not afraid to get wet and walk around in the surf like nothing matters but the boys on the beach and the golden glow of their skin. They're undamaged and uncomplicated, just looking for a good time and a pretty face to smile at over the fire.

"Do you want to take me home?" I ask, unwilling to look at him. To let him see the vulnerability in my eyes.

"No," he answers quickly, no hesitation. "I want to sit with you and have a beer."

I grin. "I think I'm good with that."

"Maybe walk down by the water."

My grin disappears. "I'm less good with that."

"Go in close. Let the waves come up and cover our feet."

"Nope."

"I wanna get you on my board and bob around out there, far away from the shore and everybody else."

I chuckle nervously. "Now you're talking crazy."

He looks at me seriously. "We'll do it before the summer is over," he promises. "We'll sit on my board and you'll put your feet in the water. I'll put my arms around you and you won't be afraid. You'll feel good because it's where you belong."

"In the ocean," I clarify slowly.

He ignores me, opening his car door and swinging his long legs outside quickly and easily. "I'll help you walk down the beach. The sand could be rough on your leg."

It's not as bad as I thought it'd be. Getting down to the beach and being on it, it doesn't kill me like I worried it would. Wyatt immediately hands me a burger, Katy gives me a hug and a beer, and they plop me down on a log on the far side of the festivities. I'm nowhere near the ocean, and even though the dark waters are coming in, sneaking up the shore like a snake in the grass, it can't get me. I'm safe.

The party is nothing exciting, but the fact that it's chill and low key is exactly why I love it and I'm glad Lawson talked me into going. I find out fast that I have a sort of celebrity status with the surfer crowd having been bitten by a shark. Everyone, guys and girls, want to see the scars, and not because they want to stare and rubberneck my pain, but because Lawson wasn't lying – scars are better seen, not heard. They share theirs with me and they ask me to tell them what I remember from what happened.

No one is more surprised than I am that I do. All it takes is three beers and one hit off the smoothest joint I've ever tasted and I'm unraveling my bandages and recounting the whole damn story.

Lawson helps me tell it, filling in the fuzzy parts, and when the bandage is off my leg he's the first to lean in close, check it out, and inform me it's 'gnarly'. His admiring tone tells me it's a compliment. His heavy, hot hand on my knee tells the other guys to look but not touch.

And I don't know if it's the beer or the weed or the way he looks by the water, but when the sun goes down and the bonfire goes up, I lean in and kiss Lawson Daniel. In front of everyone. Full on the mouth, with my tongue. With my heart in my throat. And that beautiful bastard kisses me back. No hesitation. No reservations.

He drives me home an hour later when my buzz starts to gather too many z's and I feel like I'll fall asleep on my feet. We ride with the windows down, 311 *Love Song* on the stereo, and smiles on our faces as we sing along. He has an amazing voice – deep and reverberating. Everything Lawson does is amazing. I tell him as much, making him laugh and accuse me of being high.

He's not wrong. But neither am I.

As I get out of the car smiling with cheeks that ache from a night full of the expression and a spirit that feels lighter than it has in months, I think that Lawson Daniel is absolutely fucking amazing.

CHAPTER TWELVE

Come 6 A.M. the next morning, I think Lawson Daniel is absolutely fucking evil.

"Rachel," Dad barks through my bedroom door. He pounds it once hard, rattling the wood in the frame. "You got a visitor out here."

I groan incoherently.

"Rach."

"Who is it?" I shout, my eyes still shut, my face half pressed into the pillow.

"Lawson."

I pry open one eye reluctantly. The world is shifty, wavy and rippling just outside of focus.

"No," I moan, closing my eye again.

"Rachel," Dad warns heavily, "I'm leaving for work in twenty minutes. I'm not leaving him alone in the house with you."

"We're not alone. Mom is here. And also, I'm not twelve years old. I don't need a chaperone."

He opens the door and comes inside, towering over my bed. I reopen my blurry eye and stare up at him. "Your mom sleeps like the dead and you're my daughter. You will *always* be twelve years old to me. Or six years old."

"Dad."

"Six years old and running naked through the

yard every chance you get."

"Stop. I'm up."

"Picking up dog shit and pretending it's cake. *Very* realistically pretending, if I remember right."

I throw the thin sheet off my body, bemoaning the fact that the house hasn't cooled at all overnight. "Dad, I said I'm up."

"I don't know if I do remember," he muses, heading for the door. "I'll see if your mom has some pictures to jog my memory. Maybe Lawson can help me look."

I run for the door, shoving past him. "Move it, old man!"

"Take it outside," he calls after me.

I freeze, turning to stare at him. "Take what outside exactly?"

"Your shenanigans."

"Is that... do you mean sex?" I whisper, shocked.

He glares at me. "No, I'm not telling you to go outside and have sex with Lawson Daniel."

"Then what are you talking about?"

"Shit cake," he says menacingly.

I put up my hands in surrender. "Fine, oh my God, fine! I'll tell him to get out."

It's surreal seeing Lawson in my living room. Like having the Hamburgler come to your house and hang out. Everybody knows who he is but nobody really *knows* the guy. He definitely doesn't make house calls.

He's wearing board shorts I've never seen before, a Captain America t-shirt that feels incredibly ironic, and he's carrying a small brown paper bag that's growing dark on the edges with grease.

He grins appreciatively when he sees me and I realize I've come flying out of my bedroom in nothing but running shorts I've never run in before and a tank top with no bra.

I quickly fold my arms over my chest. "What are you doing here?"

He holds out the bag to me. "I brought you breakfast."

"At six in the morning?"

"It's the most important meal of the day."

"And I'll definitely get on it in a couple hours."

"Eh," he says doubtfully, eying the grease stains on the bad. "This might have dissolved into a puddle by then. Besides, you'll miss the best waves in a couple of hours."

I shake my head. "I'm not going surfing with you."

"I didn't think you would, not yet."

"Not ever."

His grin widens. "Never say never."

"I didn't."

"I guess you didn't. But I'm not asking you to surf. I'm asking you to put your feet in the water today."

"You ask me to do a lot of things, did you notice that?"

He gestures to my clothes. "Are you ready? You're going like that?"

I half sigh, half groan and snatch the bag out of his hand. "Give me two minutes. I'll get changed."

He blinks, a little shocked. "Wow, really? I had

a whole bunch of arguments locked and loaded."

"I figured you would, so why fight it? You'd stand here trying to wear me down for the next two hours and I won't get any more sleep either way. I might as well eat this bag of lard and go with you."

"I have coffee in the car."

"You just shaved my prep time down to one minute. I'll be right out."

Lawson goes outside to the wait in the car and I run to my room to change. I don't know where Dad is, probably in the kitchen, and I'm not super eager to face him. He definitely doesn't like me even speaking to Lawson and he will absolutely hate me throwing on a bikini under my clothes and heading for the beach with him. But it's what I want to do. It's what I need to do.

When we're on our way to the beach I open the bag and find a breakfast sandwich inside. It looks homemade and when I bite into it I almost die of delicious.

"Whoa," I mutter, my mouth full of food.

Lawson looks at me with a smile. "You like it?"

"I'm in love with it. Where did you get this?"

"I made it."

"Bullshit."

"Nope. I seriously made it."

"I can't believe you cook." I take another bite, my mouth watering around the savory bit of ham, the perfectly cooked egg, and the smooth, cool flavor of avocado. "And well too."

"I'm awesome at everything, remember?"

"That was a joke last night. Today it's a matter

of fact."

He chuckles, watching me take another bite. "I'm glad you like it."

"Love it," I remind him. "I love it." I take a sip of the coffee he's brought me and nearly spit it back in the cup. "Your coffee game, however, is seriously weak."

"Yeah, that's not me. That's my stepmom."

I cringe. "Oops. Sorry."

"Don't be. It's terrible and she knows it. We all know it but we can't talk about it because she's trying to be helpful. She wakes up at dawn with me and makes us coffee while I cook breakfast."

"That's nice."

"Yeah," he says, not sounding at all convincing.

I ball up the empty paper bag, wishing it had another sandwich inside. Will he judge if I lick the bag? Probably.

"You don't like spending time with her?" I ask about his stepmom.

"It's not that. She's cool. She just tries so damn hard. She gets involved in everything we do. She wakes up with me when I get ready to surf but what I really want is to be alone. To be inside my head in silence, but she wants to talk. A lot."

"What does she want to talk about?"

"Aaron."

That name is like a bombshell. It jolts me, shakes me, throws me for a loop that I don't know how to get right from.

I lick my lips, keeping my eyes forward. "Why is she hung up on him?"

Is it for the same reason the entire town is hung up on him? Because he disappeared without a trace a year ago and you're entirely family refuses to talk about him?

"She's worried about him."

"Why?"

Lawson pulls us into the parking lot and kills the engine. We're the only ones here. The beach is covered in a fine morning fog that's slowly shifting to the north. It passes over the sand, over the car, like ghosts on parade.

"Because he won't talk about things," he says quietly, his voice deep and full of so much *something* that I feel lightheaded from the weight of it. But what 'it' is, I'm not sure.

"About things he's seen in the Navy?"

"Yeah."

"Lawson," I ask gently, my blood pounding through my veins, "did something happen to him?"

He stares out the windshield at the fog and the water and the waves. He doesn't answer me and I'm not even a hundred percent sure he heard me. Finally he runs his hand over his eyes, down onto his mouth, and blows into his palm harshly.

"It's getting late," he tells me briskly. "Let's get down there."

Lawson walks with me to the circle of logs we sat on last night by the bonfire. The place where I kissed him in front of everyone, and that reminder has me wondering when I'll get a call from Katy. Probably a little closer to a normal waking hour and I'm grateful for this small window of time where I'm free. Where it's just Lawson and I and us being whatever the hell we want to be. No questions. No expectations.

"You okay right here?" he asks, dropping his towel and already reaching up to pull his shirt off over the back of his head.

"Yeah, I'm good."

He grins, balling up his shirt in his hands. "You could always come closer. Sit by the water."

I laugh, short and unimpressed. "I could strip down naked and swim out to the middle of the ocean, but I'm not gonna do it."

"I'll do it with you."

I point to the water. "Go. Surf. This is what you drug me out of bed for, so do it."

He picks up his board and tucks it under his arm before leaning down to where I'm sitting on the log. He kisses me quickly and softly. "That's not why I brought you out here."

"Oh no? Why then?"

"Because I like having you around, Rachel."

I look at his arms but I can't tell if it happened. If he felt anything.

"Does it still do it for you saying my name like that?" I ask him. "Even after the other night?"

He stands up straight, smiling roguishly. "No. It does something way different now."

He takes off at a sprint down the beach, not bothering to give me a chance to reply and that's okay. I have no idea what I would have said to that.

He hits the water like it's not even there, running through it until he can lay on his board and start to paddle with long, strong strokes. A wave comes at him and he grabs his board, diving them under the break as one and coming up on the other side. He's out there in the calm faster than seems natural, his body made for the water. For navigating it. For riding it.

Watching Lawson surf is like listening to music. It's all about timing and balance. Just the right amount of a million different things that come together in a perfectly pitched work of art that you can't walk away from.

You see all of these surfer movies or people doing it on TV shows and they almost never wipe out. They're on their board riding in the curl like it's the easiest thing in the world, but it's not. Spend a day on the beach and watch the amateurs go at it, even the good ones, and you'll see them eat shit more times than you could ever imagine. So often you wonder why they even bother getting back up. But it's not about riding perfectly every time. Not for the ones who really love it. It's about riding that one wave in a million that you get right. That you fall in step with the ocean on and you roll together. You ride with it, not on it.

It's only the gifted few that can consistently ride the waves like they're born of them. That can feel it in the movement of the water when a wave is coming. That hear it in the sound of the spray. It's people like Lawson who make it look easy when it's anything but. What it's really like is riding a wild animal – untamed and unpredictable. You have to have the instinct to do it. You have to love the beast or she'll buck you.

I loved her once, and watching Lawson glide over the glinting blue surface, the whitewater chasing playfully at his heels, it makes me ache in my chest. It makes me long for what I've lost.

It makes me brave.

As Lawson heads out to wait for another wave, I leave the log. I walk slowly down the shore in my bare feet, the cold morning sand still wet from the high tide that's pulling out farther and farther. That's calling to me like the Pied Piper, singing and dancing so close but so far away. It feels like I have to walk miles to reach the water, but once I'm there it feels like it happened too fast. Like maybe I'm not ready after all.

My stomach knots nervously as the water rushes toward my feet. It foams and bubbles along the edges, green and golden from the sand underneath. I wait patiently, my heart sitting silent in my chest until the water reaches my toes.

Then it explodes.

My breath bursts out in a loud gasp that sounds like a laugh. My blood pours through my body until my vision is pulsing with the race of my heart and my hands press against my mouth to contain the shout that wants to scream past my lips. I want to yell at the water. I want to tell it to fuck off. To tell it it's a dick for betraying me the way it did.

And then I want to collapse inside of it. I want to be home and I want to be whole.

My body is at war with itself, a contradiction of everything, standing there a stone still, shaken mess. I want to be over it, I want to be me again, but I'm so fucking angry that I don't know if I ever will be. It's not the fear that has me frozen at the water's edge. It's the rage. The indignation at the absolute treachery I was handed.

"Is it happening?" Lawson asks, showing up out of nowhere. "Are we getting naked and swimming out?"

He's standing in water up to his knees, his board back under his arm and his body dripping wet.

"I'm pissed off," I tell him bluntly.

"At me?"

"No."

"At who then?"

"The water."

"For what?"

I scoff. "What do you think, Lawson?"

"Be mad at the shark, not the ocean. It's not the ocean's fault."

"I can't find the shark." I point to the water swirling around him. "I can find the water."

"That's not fair."

"Tell it to my leg."

"Come over here."

I frown at him. "What?"

He holds out his hand to me. "Come over here. Stand in the surf with me."

"No."

"No shark is coming up this far on the beach," he reasons patiently. "If you know it's the shark's fault and not the ocean's, then you shouldn't have a problem getting in the water."

I hesitate, my skin turning hot. "I could have drowned."

"Because the shark pulled you under. You're a strong swimmer. You were fine until he got there so again, not the water's fault. Get over here."

"You're being bossy," I stall. "Normally you ask me to do things. You don't tell me."

He sighs. "Rachel, will you please come stand in the water with me?"

"Well, since you said please."

I don't move.

"I'm missing some serious time out there," he laments.

"Then go back out."

"No."

"Why not?"

"Because this is important."

I take a deep breath and a slow step toward him.

He doesn't say a word. He doesn't even move, but the water does. It comes to greet me, slow and easy. Gentle and full of foam that tickles and pops effervescently over my skin. Up to my ankles. Then my shins. It leaves me, pulling out and taking the sand around me with it until I'm standing in a small hole created by my weight and resistance. By my reluctance. I step outside of it, moving slowly. I keep my eyes on Lawson's hand and it when I can reach it I put my palm against his just as a new wave washes over me. It reaches my shins, making me gasp, but Lawson threads his fingers through mine and he pulls me the last step toward him until I'm in it up to my thighs and my scar is almost under the water and my chest is against his, warm and wet.

He looks down at me with admiring eyes, a ghost of a grin on his lips. "You see?" he asks deeply. "You're still alive."

"I don't want to go any further," I reply rapidly.

"Okay. We won't." He squeezes my hand still clasped in his. "Thank you for coming this far."

I laugh shakily. "Thank you for getting me here."

"It feels good, doesn't it?"

The waves rush forward, knocking Lawson in the back of the legs. He's sturdy but he leans forward with the force, pushing into me. His face comes closer, his eyes look deeper, and his hold on my hand is softer. Warmer. Everything about him so strong and beautiful. So natural it's hypnotic.

"It does," I breathe, his mouth only inches away and closing. "It feels really good."

CHAPTER THIRTEEN

"You slept with him, didn't you?"

"No."

Katy raises a skeptical eyebrow but I keep my poker face. I hold my ground and I deny it, not because I'm ashamed of it but because I like it. Because I'm protecting it. I don't know what Lawson will say if one of his boys asks him if we've had sex, but judging by the fact that he didn't know I slept with Baker back in high school I'm inclined to believe they're at least a little bit mute about their extracurricular activities.

"Are you sure?"

I laugh, taking a greedy lick of my ice cream as it tries to dissolve down the side of the cone. "I think I'd know."

"That kiss on the beach was pretty legit."

"I was wasted. I barely remember it."

"You didn't seem that wasted."

"That's because I'm better at it than you are."

Katy's shoulders sag. "Are you really going to bring this up again?'

I smile. "I'm never going to let you forget it."

"Fine, whatever."

"Sophomore year. Behind the football field in the woods. Mac Gibson, or Ol' Mac Donghold as he was known to some for mysterious and probably disgusting reasons. A four pack of wine coolers and a full pack of cigarettes."

"Are you enjoying yourself?" she asks blandly.

"Shh, this is my favorite part," I whisper before raising my voice way too loud. "You, Katelin Reynolds, were nearly caught rounding second base with Ol' Mac Donghold when he heard the fuzz coming. He, the brave and chivalrous boy that he was, ran into the woods and left you behind. You, being utterly wasted and totally shitty at it, cried, vomited, got caught, and spent the majority of that summer grounded in your room. Did I miss any of it?"

Katy stabs her hot fudge sundae angrily. "Mac ran away with my bra and showed it to the whole school the next day," she mumbles.

"Mac ran away with your bra and showed it to the entire school the very next day," I announce loudly.

Heads turn. Kids giggle. Mother's frown. Mac's dad glares at me from his place in line at the Frosty Freeze register.

"Fucking small towns," I grumble under my breath.

Katy laughs, her mood instantly lighter. "Serves you right."

"Yeah, yeah."

"How's the job going? Are you saving up enough for the plane ticket?"

I groan in annoyance. "I think so, but I lost my deposit on the apartment I had set up. I'll have to find a new one along with a fresh deposit." I reach over and throw my melting ice cream into the trash, giving up. My hands are coated in an invisible stickiness that I brush at fruitlessly with a brown napkin. "It seems like every time I think I'm done paying for what happened something else comes up. I'm starting to wonder if I shouldn't just say screw it and wait another year."

"You can't do that," Katy tells me seriously. "You already put it off for two years after we graduated. If you put it off again you'll never go and you *have* to go."

"Why? What's the point?"

"The point is you're good!"

"And the other students there will be better."

"So what? If you're not the best you're not gonna go?"

I shrug, looking out the window. "I don't know."

"Big fish in a little pond?" she asks knowingly. "Scared of being the little fish in the big pond?"

"Something like that."

"Well, if you need to talk about it I know just the person you should go to. Kind of an expert on the subject."

I turn to her, my brows pinched in confusion. "Who?"

She laughs, kicking me gently under the table. "Lawson Daniel, dummy."

"I can't bring this up with him."

"Oh, okay. You can share saliva with him but you can't talk to him?"

"We talk."

"About what? How hot he is? How he wants to

do you? His favorite yoga pose on a surfboard? Is it downward facing dolphin? Tell me it's downward facing dolphin."

"No," I laugh.

"No it's not or no you won't tell me."

"No, to everything."

"Even sleeping with him?"

"Ugh, let it go."

"Not until you let Mac Donghold go."

I smile, shaking my head vehemently. "Never."

***

The room is cool. It's dry and dark, the outside world kept out. Kept locked away behind the curtained windows that let in little shafts of light speckled with clusters of dust kicked up by my fingers flying over the keys. An old xylophone sits silently in the corner, it's golden wood notched and abused. A set of drums worn white by countless palms percussing its surface stands still. Listening. The entire room is listening, absorbing as I play. As I pour myself into the song. As I give it everything I have and come up short.

"Holy shit."

My fingers stumble, my timing thrown off and my focus gone.

I spin on the stool to shout at whoever burst in and startled me, but my anger dies on my lips when I meet his eyes.

"Sorry," Lawson apologizes immediately. He stands straight, pulling himself up from where he was leaning against the doorframe. "I kept my mouth shut as long as I could. But holy shit."

"What are you doing here?"

Only a faint light is coming in from the hallway behind him, his face almost entirely cast in shadow, but I catch the flicker of a grin on his lips. "Believe it or not, your dad told me where I could find you. I think he did it just to get me off his property."

"I doubt that was it," I assure him, completely sure that it is.

He moves slowly into the room, circling wide. "You don't have to lie. Dad's don't like me. It's no secret."

"He should at least wait to get to know you before he hates you."

"He thinks he already does." He stops on the opposite side of the gleaming black piano, one of the only instruments in the music room that's undamaged, and puts his palms on the surface. "It's creepy being back here."

"It's an elementary school," I chuckle. "How creepy can it be?"

"How often do you come here?"

"Often. I've been coming here after hours since the fourth grade to practice."

"I'm surprised you don't have a piano at home."

I hover my head over the keys, hiding behind my hair. "No, we do. The acoustics are better in here, though. And I play the same thing over and over again for hours. It gets irritating for anyone else in the house."

And the piano my parents spent the entire household Christmas fund on six years ago is old and always out of tune.

"What were you playing just now?" Lawson asks. "It sounded complicated."

I laugh, nodding my head. "It is. It's not an easy one. It's Schumann. *Fantasie.*" I drag my fingers unceremoniously over the keys, sending a string of nonsense through the air. "I'm not good at it."

"It sounded good to me."

"Because you've never heard it played well before. I'm clumsy with it. I get distracted, I dismantle the tempo. It throws everything off."

"Distracted by what?"

"The song. The story."

"It has a story?"

I grin at him. "All music has a story."

He smiles, taking a seat in a metal chair to my right and leaning forward on his elbows. "What's this one about?"

"Schumann was in love with a girl. She was nine years younger than him but a piano prodigy. They fell in love. Her parents didn't approve."

"Lot of that going around," Lawson says dryly.

"Ha ha," I laugh theatrically. "Anyway, they wouldn't let them see each other so he wrote her music with hidden messages. *Fantasie* was one of them. It was a love letter. One she could play over and over again, knowing it was for her. When she turned eighteen he proposed, she accepted, her parents said no, and they sued them for the right to get married. A judge gave them the go ahead and so they did."

"It's a nice story. I can see why you like the

song."

"Yeah, well, *that* part is nice. Eventually Schumann tried to commit suicide, was tossed into a mental hospital, and died."

"Oh."

"Yeah. But the song is good, right?"

He frowns. "I don't know anymore."

"Yeah," I sigh. "Me either."

"Play me something else."

"What do you want to hear?"

"What do you want to play?"

"*Fantasie*. Flawless."

"No. What do you like to play? What makes this fun for you?"

I stop to think, absently plucking at the keys as I do.

I look at Lawson. At his patient face, dark and daring in this space. Invading it and making it his. Taking it and giving it back to me better than it was before. He carries this unfailing peace, a natural calm he learned from the sea. A certainty he has in his heart that he's trying so hard to teach to me and I remember it in the feel of his hand on mine by the water. I clung to it. I needed it, needed him, to survive.

My fingers start to move, my mind made up before I know it. Before I realize what I'm doing.

What I'm saying without uttering a word.

I play *Stay With Me* by Sam Smith. And I play it for Lawson.

I close my eyes, playing from memory and making up the rest as I go. I take it and mold it, make it mine, give it life and form and I don't give a damn about the rules because there are none. I'm lawless. Weightless. Unfettered and flying, and when he starts to sing along, his beautifully rich voice filling the room, I feel myself start to slip.

I'm sliding under the surface. I'm stepping deeper into the water with him, going past my knees, past my waist. It's up to my chest, to my heart, and it's filling it, flooding it.

And as afraid as I am, I'm not fighting it.

When the song is over, when my fingers have gone still and my heart is barely beating, I open my eyes.

He's there. He's in front of me and he doesn't hesitate to lift me up off the stool as though I weigh nothing and put me carefully down on the flat top of the piano. His hips are between my thighs, his hands rising up my ribs, and I don't hesitate to descend my mouth to his. To devour him, taking with my tongue as he takes with his hands, filling them with my body as I pass each shuddered, desperate breath I take into his mouth. As I pull air from his lungs to fill my own.

He works his magic, my clothes disappearing instantly along with his until we're all heat and heart, skin and sweat pulling and pushing in all the right places. He moves me back, lowering me until I'm lying flat against the piano. His hands ride up my stomach to my chest, soothing my skin and bringing my blood to a boil. Then he chases them with his lips. With his tongue.

The way he plays me, I'm sure he could play *Fantasie* to a T. Every note, every chord, plucked to perfection.

I stretch my arms high over my head, curling my fingers around the edge of the piano top, my legs still draped around his hips on the opposite side.

"Lawson," I moan, unable to hold it inside.

My body arches, bowing at the waist, and he runs his arm under it to keep me that way. To line me up with his body, ready to play the finale.

"Say it again, Rachel," he murmurs, his lips against the sensitive skin of my stomach. "Say my name again."

"Lawson," I sigh.

He groans, his mouth racing up my body between my breasts as he slides inside me.

It's not the way it was before. It's faster, harder, more aggressive and more grappling, but it's the same song in a different key. I still know it. I still recognize it, and the way we play it together is better than anything I've ever known. It's tender and raucous. It's sweet and desperate.

It's Lawson and I.

CHAPTER FOURTEEN

"Why did you never go pro?"

Lawson stops, his chopsticks holding the fat piece of sushi just outside the reach of his lips.

When we left the music room – running and giggling like kids – Lawson insisted on buying me dinner. He also insisted that he knew a bar in Santa Barbara with the best sushi on the coast. I didn't believe him because bars are great for greasy burgers and cheddar cheese fries, but a good squid nigiri? Not likely.

I was wrong. I was so friggin' wrong. And I ate my words with a side of the tastiest cucumber roll I've ever had.

Lawson finally lowers his hand, giving me his full attention. "Why didn't I move up to pro surfing?"

"Yeah. Unless that's too personal a question."

I'm relieved when he smiles. "After what we just did, there's not much I'd put in the 'too personal' column for us."

"Okay," I agree with a grin. "So then why?"

He shrugs, leaning forward over his food and poking it with his chopsticks. "Bad timing, I guess."

"I heard you were being recruited by a sponsor right out of high school."

"Middle school," he corrects.

"And in all these years it's never been the right time to live your dream?"

"Who said it was my dream?"

"I don't know. Everyone in town?"

He looks up at me from under his eyelashes. "And people in town know everything, don't they?"

I smile, conceding the point. "Alright, so we all got you wrong. About a lot of things."

"Almost everything."

"Please. You love to surf. You love to fool around with girls. You love to smoke pot. You love to drink."

"That's a strong word. I've done all of that but I wouldn't say I love any of it but surfing. The rest is just filler. Filler that I don't do as often as everyone thinks I do."

"Filler for what?"

"Time." He smiles at me lazily, but I can see something else there. Something just below the surface that he's hiding. "I'm just passing the time, Rachel."

"You never answered my question."

"Which one?"

"Why you didn't go pro."

He forces a frown. "I thought I did."

"No," I reply solidly. "You evaded it and gave me the runaround, something you're very good at, by the way. But you never answered me."

He sits back in his seat and stretches his arms over the back of the booth in both directions. His wing span is large, eating the entire space and that coupled with his easy grin reminds me of a big bird of prey. But the guarded look in his eyes is that of the beautiful exotic that darts and weaves, never trusting. Always a blur. Never standing still long enough to be seen.

Lawson is a lot of things, and I'm starting to see that none of them are exactly what everyone assumes.

"I didn't go pro right out of middle school because I didn't want to be a drop out," he explains evenly. "If I signed with a sponsor I'd be doing advertising and interviews, events and competitions all over the world, all year long. I couldn't finish school. I'd have to get a GED and that might be fine for some people, but not me. I wanted to finish high school the right way with the people I grew up with. So I said no to the sponsor. I told them I wasn't ready to go pro until I finished high school. They said good luck and moved on to the next guy."

"And they never came calling again? Not even when you finished high school? You still win every competition you go into. They have to know about you."

"They do and yeah, they called. Last year the guy they signed instead of me blew his knee out in a dirt bike accident. He's wrecked, he can't stand on a board anymore so they were looking for a new poster boy."

"They called you?"

"They called me. And I said yes."

I shake my head, confused. "If you said yes a year ago, what are you still doing here? Shouldn't you be in Africa or Tahiti right now?"

He lowers his arms, reaching for his beer. "Bad

timing, remember?"

And then it hits me – they called a year ago.

Aaron fell off the radar almost exactly one year ago.

"You didn't go because of Aaron," I say softly, afraid to speak the name too loudly. Afraid to ruffle his feathers.

Lawson only nods, his eyes vacantly fixed on his plate.

"Where is he, Lawson?"

He surprises me when he laughs shortly. "Right now? Uh, probably in the basement getting caught up on Game of Thrones."

"The basement where?"

"At home."

I gape at him. "Are you shitting me? Aaron is in Isla Azul?"

He watches me closely, his face calm but his eyes churning anxiously. "He has been for months."

"Are you shitting me?!"

People all over the dimly lit bar turn to look at us. Tuesday drinkers, people who don't care about jobs or hangovers anymore, all looking at us in irritation for harshing their mellow.

Lawson puts his drink down and leans forward on the table. "Shh," he hisses quietly. "Keep your voice down."

"Are you shitting me?" I whisper shout at him, leaning forward as well. "Aaron Daniel is in Isla Azul?

"Yes."

"How long?"

"Over six months."

"Lawson Daniel," I scold quietly.

"You can't tell anyone."

I slap his shoulder hard.

"Ow! What was that for?" he demands, rubbing his shoulder.

"You don't tell someone something like that and wait until *after* to swear them to secrecy, you dick."

"Either way, you can't tell anyone. Especially Katy. It's a secret."

"No duh it's a secret. It's the biggest secret in town. Katy is my best friend and you're telling me that I can't tell her that the love of her life is alive and living less than three miles away?"

Lawson's brows fall. "He was the love of her life?"

"Still is."

"I didn't know. I thought it was just a summer fling."

"It lasted longer than the summer."

"I know, but still. I didn't know."

I take a breath, recovering from the shock and my anger at the muzzle he immediately slapped on me. "Does he ever ask about her?"

"No," he answers bluntly. "He doesn't talk about much of anything but what an inbred piece of shit Joffrey is."

"Am I allowed to ask the million dollar question?"

"Go for it."

"Why is he hiding?"

"I can't tell you."

I slap his shoulder again. Harder this time.

He flinches, grinning slightly.

"You're an asshole," I curse him vehemently. "Why would you tell me all of that if I'm not allowed to tell anyone else?"

"Because I haven't been allowed to tell anyone. Not even the guys. No one's been over to the house since Aaron got back and the only people I can even mention it to are Candace or my dad, and not even them sometimes."

"Why not?"

"Candace is going insane over it. She's not sleeping, she barely eats."

"Why is she so stressed?"

"Because she's a stepmom and she knows it. It's been seven years and she's still convinced she's gotta win us over. She goes crazy over everything." He points to a faint white scar along his hairline by his temple. "I came home with a little gash on my head and she rushed me to the hospital. They put Bactine and a bandage on it. It was embarrassing. And with what happened to Aaron... she's fuckin' manic."

"You're not gonna tell me what happened to him, are you?"

"No."

"Dick."

He chuckles, taking a sip of his beer.

"I'm glad you told me."

"Really?" Lawson asks me skeptically. "Because the ache in my shoulder says you're not."

"You puss. I barely touched you."

"You have a sledgehammer for a hand."

I laugh, reaching for his hand and running my

fingertips along the inside of his palm. "You're a big boy. You can take it."

He clenches his hand around mine, pulls it up to his lips, and kisses my knuckles softly.

The gesture is quick but sweet, sending a flourish of butterflies wild inside me.

"So what about you?" he asks suddenly. "You've been playing piano as long as I've been surfing. Why'd you wait two years to go to school for it?"

I gently pull my hand back, my smile fading with the butterflies and the heat of his skin. "I didn't wait. I applied during our senior year of high school. I didn't get it."

"Shit, I'm sorry, Rach."

"No, it's okay. It hurt, it was hard, but I decided to take two years to practice, get my Associates Degree, and then last December I applied again." I give him a weak smile. "This time I got in."

"Will your credits transfer to NEC?"

I chuckle, shaking my head. "Not really, but that's okay. I think it was worth it."

"You got your Associates out of it. Definitely not time wasted," he agrees.

"If you're not going pro with surfing do you ever think about going to college?"

"I did."

"What?" I balk. "When?"

He smiles at my reaction, bringing his beer to his lips. "Same as you. Right out of high school. Two years."

"What did you study?"

"Computers."

"Wow," I mutter. "That is *so* not what I expected you to say."

"Well, they don't give out degrees in man-whoring and pot smoking," he tells me sardonically. "I checked."

"You're hilarious."

"Is that what you've heard?"

"Alright, alright," I laugh. "You got a bad rap. I admit it. On behalf of all of Isla Azul, I am sorry we misjudged you."

Lawson reaches forward with his beer bottle and taps it to my head and both shoulders. "You're forgiven."

"Thank you," I say with a small bow. "So why computers? What do you want to do with them?"

"I'm already doing it. I'm a freelance graphic designer. I do webpages, logos, short videos. I bought an underwater camera that I can mount to my board. I take shots of the ocean when I'm surfing. Only about one in a thousand is really worth anything but I sell them to other websites. I'm earning royalties off printings of a few."

"Wow, Lawson, congratulations," I tell him ardently. "That's... it's amazing. Why doesn't anyone in town know about this?"

He eyes me seriously, his voice deep and quiet when he speaks. "Because it's not filler, and I don't give that town anything but filler."

"Then why are you giving it to me?"

"Because, Rachel Mason," he says with a cautious smile, "you are quickly becoming my favorite person on the planet."

CHAPTER FIFTEEN

For the Fourth of July Lawson says he has a surprise for me. He asks me to wear my red bikini, the one with the American flag on the right breast, and I wonder again at how well he knows my wardrobe. But I wear it for him and I don't complain.

We leave early in the morning because Lawson knows no other time of day than really freakin' early, and he drives us south down the coast. Katy and Wyatt sit in the back seat, the rest of his boys in Xander's old blue Jeep Wrangler cruising behind us. It's only fifteen minutes into the drive when Katy falls asleep in the backseat. When I look back her head is resting on Wyatt's lap, his long, tan fingers slowly threading through her hair. He smiles at me when I catch him, but he doesn't stop and I swear I've never seen a guy look happier than he does in that moment.

I wish Katy could see it too. I wish she could see a lot of things about Wyatt, but she doesn't and that's not her fault. It's not Wyatt's either. I don't know for sure it's Aaron's but I do know he's not helping.

"Are you taking me to work?" I ask Lawson when we pull down the main strip Ambrose Surf sits on. "Is that my surprise? Cause it sucks."

He laughs, shaking his head. "No, store is closed. We're going somewhere nearby, though. To a house party."

"I'm not doing a keg stand."

"It's not that kind of house party."

"What kind is it?"

Lawson only smiles.

Five minutes later I find out – it's the swanky kind. He parks us on the street in front of a row of houses sitting on the beach. They're right up against the water, each one with access out its back door to the surf, and I know for a fact that in Malibu not a single one of these could cost less than a few million dollars.

"Whose house is this party at?" Katy asks groggily, emerging slowly from the back seat.

Lawson goes to the back of the car and opens the hatch to pull out our bags. "It's Don's place."

"My boss Don?" I ask doubtfully.

"Yep. The Double D himself."

I freeze. "Wait."

Lawson closes the trunk, smiling at me. "You recognize it now?"

"Whoa."

"Whoa what?" Katy asks, looking between the two of us. She glances at Wyatt to find him smiling as well. "What am I missing?"

"Double D was huge in the eighties," I tell her. "They show his old footage in every surfing highlight reel. They made an entire documentary about him that Dad made me watch about a million times. No one could ride like him."

"They still can't," Lawson agrees.

I look at him impatiently. "Some people definitely can."

"Don't tell him that."

"My dad will die when I tell him I work for Double D." My shoulders slump unhappily. "Wait, it's not a secret is it?"

"He's not Superman," Wyatt says with a chuckle. "Why would it be a secret?"

"Because Lawson is a dick."

Lawson laughs. He slings his arm over my shoulders and leads us toward the house. "No, it's not a secret. You can tell your dad. Bring him into the shop, Don would love to talk to him if he's a surfing fan. He likes when the older crowd comes in."

"I thought I was there to help draw in the young guys."

"You are. Young guys are the ones doing most of the buying. I don't know if you've noticed, but Don likes to do a lot of talking. The old guys like to talk, not buy."

"They also like to look."

"At you or the boards?"

I reach over and pinch his side. He yelps, jumping away from me.

"What was that for?"

I roll my eyes. "Give me some credit, Lawson. I'm not exactly a super model but I like to think I'm more interesting to a man than a surfboard."

"Depends on the board."

I lunge at him, ready to pinch him again but he's too fast. He rushes away from me toward the front door and bursts inside to safety. And I would keep after him, but when I step inside I'm floored.

The view is amazing. Floor to ceiling windows span the entire western side of the house. A big open living room with slouching couches covered in overstuffed cushions stare out over the water. A gleaming stainless steel kitchen is nestled in the corner to the right, a long black bar stretching out beside it. People mill around everywhere, bare feet tracking sand all over the rich dark wood flooring that covers every square inch of this level, continuing up the stairs and probably across the second floor as well.

And the air. Oh the sweet, savory feel of air conditioning swirling around my legs and up over my bare arms. It gets in my hair and makes me sigh as I stare out the massive windows to the waves rolling in white and foaming.

"Holy shit," I mumble, walking numbly to stand next to Lawson. "Don is Iron Man."

"You mean Tony Stark?"

"I mean shut up, this house is insane." I turn to Lawson, my mouth still hanging open in amazement. I can't control it. I've lost all bodily control. "How can he afford this? Can you make that much money as a pro surfer?" I whisper.

Lawson laughs. "Not often. Most of this is paid for by the shop."

"The shop. The surf shop that I work in? The one with only one bathroom marked neither women's or men's but simply 'Hang Loose' and a toilet you have to manually refill the tank on? That surf shop?"

"He's selective on what he'll spend his money on." He points to the front row seat to the ocean. "The water he cares about. His boards, his store, his merchandise, his employees – they all matter. Plumbing doesn't do it for him."

"He's loaded though, isn't he?"

"Oh yeah. Massively. He does custom work for a lot of people, a lot of pros. He got in early with a guy back in the nineties making board wax and that blew up big. It's everywhere now."

"Dee's Wax?" I ask, picturing the small tin circle with the sunshine yellow writing sitting by the register.

"That's it. He has other shops too. Florida, Hawaii, Tahiti. He's opening one in Australia next year. Wherever the pros go, Don goes."

"I had no idea. I thought it was just another surf shop."

"Nope. It's *the* surf shop." He nudges me with a smile. "You probably met a pro or two, you just didn't know it."

"Have you met pros in there?"

"Yeah, I know a few."

"You know them? As in you talk to them outside the store?"

"Sure. I have Rob Machado on speed dial."

I narrow my eyes at him. "See, I don't know if you're kidding or not."

He grins but he doesn't answer.

***

We spend the majority of the day by the water.

I even spend some of it *in* the water. I never get in so far that I can't touch the bottom, but it feels good to do it. To body surf with Katy. To wade in the surf with Lawson.

He isn't shy about me, and I'm amazed by how much that amazes me. There are other surfers here, a lot of other women, but Lawson makes it very clear from the moment we get here that I'm with him. His arm is around my shoulders or his hand is holding mine. He's standing behind me with his hand resting possessively on my hip. He's in the water with his lips against mine, his tongue taking control. The more the day goes on, the more beers he has, the more brazen he is. His hands linger longer, they drift higher. He pulls me to him closer. Harder. He whispers in my ear things both sweet and sultry. He tells me I'm beautiful. He tells me he loves being with me. He tells me all the things he wishes he could do to me if we were alone.

"He is so into you," Katy tells me as we sit on our towels watching the boys surf.

I sigh. "Don't," I warn her. "Please don't do that."

"Do what? Do you see the way he looks at you? And he can't keep his hands off you."

"I know."

"Tell me again how you guys haven't slept together. I love that one. It's hilarious."

"Yes, fine, we slept together."

She looks at me sideways, waiting silently.

"A couple of times," I admit.

"Was it good?"

"What do you think?"

"I think that boy is crazy about you."

"No. That's just how he is. It's how he acts with girls."

"I've never seen him with a girl the way he is with you. And we've all seen him with *a lot* of girls." She pauses, chewing on the inside of her cheek thoughtfully. "Trust me," she says softly, "I know what I'm talking about. I know what a Daniel boy in love looks like."

And there it is. There *he* is. Always. The man who loved her, made her love him, and left her high and dry without a word. Without a hope. With nothing but a scar on her heart and a pain that won't go away. It's not what I want. It's not where I want to be and if I'm not very careful it's exactly where I'll land.

"I just… I like him," I admit on an exhale. "I really, really like him, Katy. He's smart and funny and talented. He's sweet, too, and seriously, would you look at him? He's so gorgeous it's scary. It should be against the law to be that good looking."

"Okay, so you like him and he likes you, and the problem is…"

"I'm trying to make it out of this alive. He doesn't do relationships and I'm leaving at the end of the summer. He's definitely not going to do a long distance one. And we've never even talked about what we're doing. We're just kind of doing it and that's part of the beauty of it. There are no rules, no expectations. We're… floating, and I like it that way."

"You like dodging decisions," Katy muses dryly. "Shocking."

I scowl at her. "What is that supposed to mean?"

"Nothing. This is smart. You're right." She stands, swiping sand off her butt. "Let it run its course. I'm sure it won't end badly for anyone."

"Are you mad at me for something?"

"Nope. I love you. I love everything about you, but I need a beer. You want one?"

"Yeah, I guess," I reply cautiously.

"What kind?"

"Whatever you can find."

She shakes her head, obviously frustrated. "That's exactly my point," she mutters before disappearing up into the house.

CHAPTER SIXTEEN

Lawson towers over me, his shadow casting long and dark over the golden sand set fire by the fading sun.

"I want you on the water," he tells me seriously.

I blink up at him. "Sorry, what?"

"You and me. On the water for the fireworks. It's happening."

"No, it's not," I laugh.

He kneels down until we're eye to eye, his body dripping water on the end of my towel. "Yes, it is. You need to do it, but mostly *I* need you to do it. With me. Right now."

I hesitate, my heart slowing dangerously. "What exactly are we talking?"

"Getting on my surfboard and getting out there on the water. Past the break."

"In the dark?"

"Yes."

"Lawson, it's not—"

He leans in until we're nose to nose. Until he's all I can see – sea green eyes and the darkest, longest lashes imaginable. His breath smells like beer but his eyes are sharp. Focused. "Do you trust me?" he asks quietly.

I take a thin, painful breath. "Yes."

"Then do this with me."

"No."

"Do it *for* me."

I purse my lips nervously. "N—"

He sits back abruptly, standing and offering me his hand. "Before you say no, come with me. You still need your surprise."

I reluctantly reach for him. His hand is strong around mine. Reassuring and terrifying at the same time. He leads me down the beach to the side of the house. There's a shed there with grey barn doors and chipped white trim. Lawson pulls one door open, then pulls me inside.

It's dark. There's not much day left and it's lost entirely inside these walls. I hold Lawson's hand harder, following him deeper inside the dark and praying I don't trip on something sharp. He mutters something about the light, about never being able to find it, and suddenly there's a *click* overhead and the room starts to glow. The bulb hanging from the ceiling takes its time to get going. It illuminates the room by degrees and I start to realize we're not alone.

Carefully stacked against every wall, standing sentinel like soldiers waiting to go to war, are surf boards of all different sizes and colors. Longboards and body boards in a rainbow array of hues. And each one has the same logo on it. The same seventies style wave sectioned into three different shades of blue with a big, bold 'A' positioned in the tube. It's the same logo on the front of Ambrose Surf.

"These are all Don's?" I ask Lawson quietly.

I keep my voice hushed because I can feel it – this is a sanctuary. This is a place of reverence for these men. These athletes and artists. These boards are family, friends that they've spent countless hours with. Every one of them has a story. Has a personality. Each of them has meaning.

Even to me.

She stands out against the rest. She's not upright, not standing tall and waiting for the chance to run to action. She's laying down and hanging high, white as snow. A sleeping beauty unable to wake.

"Layla," I whisper in shock.

Lawson takes a step toward her. He uses two hands to carefully lift her from the hooks holding her up and brings her down for me to see. For me to touch if I want to.

"After what happened I knew I'd never ride her again," Lawson explains. "Like I told you, her vibe changed after that day. I'd never be able to be out on her without thinking of you and what happened. I didn't want it to scare me off. I didn't want to get cautious."

"Why is she at Don's?"

"Because he wouldn't let me get rid of her for good. He said things change. People heal." Lawson stands her up next to him, his hand running down the surface and a smile playing on his lips in the low glow of the room. "He knew that this was *my* board. He promised to keep her for me until I was ready to ride her again."

"And you think you're ready?"

"No." He looks at me seriously, his eyes imploring. He's not telling. He's asking. He's nearly pleading. "I think *we're* ready."

I fight the urge to shake my head. To tell him no and leave that room, maybe even that beach. I've made a lot of progress lately. I was in the water today up to my neck and I didn't panic and die. It's only been a month. What does he expect from me? What does he want?

"I've asked you not to thank me," he reminds me.

I laugh shakily. "And you want this instead."

"Yeah."

"You're blackmailing me again."

"Yeah."

"Why do I have to go with you? Can't you ride her by yourself?"

"No."

I raise my eyebrows expectantly. "That's it? That's your argument?"

He grins. "Yeah."

"Lawson," I sigh reluctantly.

He steps forward, one hand on his board and his other on my face and his lips against mine, hot and earnest. He kisses me deeply, slowly, until my hands are on his waist to steady me and my breathing is slowed to almost nothing. Until we're both breathless and burning.

"Rachel," he says roughly, quietly.

I don't know if it does anything to him to say my name anymore, but it does something to me to hear it. It lights me up inside, slow like the light. Growing and growing, warming and filling the empty spaces, the dark corners. He heals me, he illuminates me. He makes me golden. And I know I him this. I owe myself this, I owe her this.

I reach out with shaking fingers until I feel the board. The roughness of the wax. Of the sand from its last ride. It feels warm under my fingertips, somehow still covered in summer sun despite being locked away and hidden from its rays.

Lawson holds me close with one arm, both of us loosely clutching Layla, and when he breaks away to look down into my eyes I don't have to tell him yes. He already knows. He can read it in my face. In my touch. He can read me the way he reads the waves.

And the smile he gives me in reply is absolutely everything.

***

We bob on the water, the dark liquid reaching up and coating my legs. Coating his. It touches my scar and retreats, comes back to kiss it again before disappearing shyly. It tickles and makes me smile and a small amount of my absolute terror dissolves in its wake.

True to his word weeks ago, Lawson sits close behind me and wraps his arms around my waist. And just as he promised, I feel safe. I feel good because it's where I belong. On the ocean. With him.

"Thank you," he murmurs in my ear.

I smile into the growing darkness. "I'll say you're welcome to close the conversation, but don't ever thank me again, okay?"

I can feel his chuckle through his body against my back. "Okay."

Laughter ripples out across the water. A splash as someone topples drunkenly off their board. The water is full of other surfers, some with their girl's on their board in front of them the way Lawson and I are. The sun is gone, the last of its burn fading out under the horizon, and we're all eagerly waiting for the fireworks to start.

I'm shaking slightly. It's not the cool of the water or the dropping temperature of the coming night. It's the déjà vu. It's the time of day when I nearly died and that fact is not lost on me. But I'm trying to keep my cool because I want to be okay. I want to be in this moment and not fear it. I want to love it.

"Are you okay?" he asks me, his arms tightening around my body.

"I think so."

"That's the problem. You're thinking too much. You're thinking about that night, aren't you?"

"Aren't you?" I challenge.

I feel him shake his head before resting his chin on my shoulder. "I'm thinking about right now. I'm thinking about you in that bikini. I'm thinking about the way the water looks on your skin. The way you smell like coconut. The way you taste when I kiss you. How dark your hair is when it's wet." He runs his palms across my stomach, fanning them out and tickling my sides. His lips fall to my shoulder where he kisses me softly. "How absolutely fucking beautiful you are in the water."

I lean back against him, laying my hands on his thighs. I'm not surprised by his touch. It's been building all day and as anxious as I am, as wound tightly as my body is, I want him to soothe it. I want him to make this better. Easier. I want to be free.

I focus on the feel of the contoured planes of his chest, wet and slick against my back. The slow rhythm of his stomach as he breathes. The hard push of him building between his legs.

His mouth becomes more brave, his tongue dancing across my skin and tasting the salt lingering there. I breathe slowly as his hands move lower. Deeper. My legs are spread by the board and when his fingers find the inside of my thighs, when they trace higher to the edge of my bikini bottom, I gasp sharply.

"People can see us," I whisper, the words not exactly a protest.

He shakes his head. "It's too dark. They can't see anything."

Lawson pushes aside my swimsuit, delving his fingers underneath and immediately I'm clenching my hands on his thighs and rolling my head back against his shoulder. He moves slowly, methodically. He listens to the notes I play in the back of my throat and matches my rhythm, a perfect harmony that makes me blind and shaky. The rocking of the board is pressing him against me and he groans and grinds, taking as he's giving. Shuddering with a moan when my hand reaches around behind me to take hold of him.

Suddenly the night explodes in fire and light.

White sparks, blue flame, and a shimmering sky of color reflecting off the water as a loud crack breaks above us. We're surrounded by people staring up at the sky, watching the fireworks as they illuminate the night as though it were day, but we don't stop. I never want this to stop. He's building the tempo, demanding I follow. He's racing us forward, entering the curl, and the wave is crashing down around us with such force that I can't even find my voice to scream when it all comes to a head.

I let it overtake me. I let it pull me under, and he holds me as it does, as we're both gasping and gulping for air. He whispers to me, sweet and low, promising to keep me afloat. To help me home.

As the world erupts and disintegrates around us, he promises to stay with me.

CHAPTER SEVENTEEN

Lawson keeps driving me to work for the next few weeks even though my leg is healing. I'm strong enough to drive and walk without help. I don't even limp. It gets tired easily but the infection is long gone and my skin is carefully knitting itself back together.

The scar is for real. My leg will never look the same, not without a shitload of money and some good plastic surgery, but I'm not vain enough for that. Despite the heat and the overwhelming desire I have to wear nothing at all on my body, I buy capris and knee length skirts to cover my thigh. I do it because I don't like to talk about it and I really don't like when people stare at it, but if one of the guys down at Ambrose asks to see it, I'm not above showing it off. It's different down there. It feels like it did on the beach with the surfers who admired it and saw it as a badge of honor instead of a disfigurement or a tragedy they're glad they were able to avoid. They have much less of a 'better her than me' attitude about it and I kind of love them for that.

Lawson and I don't question it that he picks me up every morning that I work. We don't even discuss the fact that he's on my doorstep at 6 a.m.

TRACEY WARD

with a brown paper bag and a crappy coffee on my days off. It's natural to us. It's become our new normal, like music and surfing. Like sex and sleeping under the stars.

But not to everyone. Not to the rest of the town. Not to Katy or my mom, and definitely not to my dad.

"He still won't let Lawson in the house in the morning," I mention to Mom as we cook dinner together.

She smiles, sweat glistening on her lip. She reaches up and pushes her hair away from her forehead with the back of her hand. "I know. I told him not to."

"What? Why?"

"Because he's Lawson Daniel."

"Don't say his name like that," I mumble irritably.

"Like what?"

"Like it's a bad thing."

"Ooh," she pokes me in the side with her elbow, "you like him."

Shit.

I shrug, leaning over the counter where I'm cutting peppers and avoiding her eager eyes. "He's a cool guy," I say indifferently.

"That's not what I've heard."

"Well, you can't believe everything you hear. Sometimes you have to find things out for yourself."

I can feel her watching me out of the corner of her eye. "I guess you're right," she eventually agrees.

We eat dinner without Dad. He's pulling another double shift down at the garage and won't be home until late. We'll have a beer and a plate of kebabs waiting for him but he'll probably fall asleep halfway through both, his feet propped up on the couch and his hat pulled low over his tired eyes. It's the ritual that's been in place all summer, longer than my ritual with Lawson, and I wish I could do something about it. I wish I could give them my paychecks. I wish I could buy them a new air conditioner. I wish I could talk him out of working these doubles to help pay my tuition so I don't sink so deeply into debt with student loans, but they'd never let me. Everything they've done since the moment I showed talent playing piano has been to foster that gift. To pave the way for me to live my dream.

I don't know how to tell them all I dream about lately is the green glow of the ocean and the cool breath of air conditioning.

The next morning Lawson is at my door, bright and early. He stands just at the edge of the threshold like a vampire waiting for admittance, an easy smile on his face.

"You ready to surf?" he asks hopefully.

I nab my breakfast out of his hand. "I'm ready to watch."

"Surfing is not a spectator sport. Neither is life. You gotta get back in the game eventually."

"Oh my God," I laugh. "Take it easy, Yoda. It's still early. I need coffee before I can take your pep talks seriously."

"It's extra bad today. She took a stab at ice

coffee because of the heat."

"Fantastic. I can't wait."

"You could stay," a voice says from behind me.

I turn around to find my mom standing in the living room. I'm amazed she's awake this early and even more amazed to find her dressed and ready for the world. She is *not* an early bird.

"Mom, what are you doing up?"

"Taking your advice." She looks over my head to Lawson, casting him a warm smile. "Come on in, Lawson. I'll make you both coffee if you agree to make me one of those breakfast sandwiches she keeps gloating about."

"We don't have time. He likes to get there early for the morning waves."

"Do you have avocado and olive oil?" he asks my mom.

"I do," she answers.

"Sausage patties, cheese, and English muffins?"

"All of it."

"You got a deal."

Mom disappears into the kitchen to start the coffee.

I round on Lawson, looking at him incredulously. "Aren't you the guy who bitched at me earlier this week for taking the time to brush my teeth and, quote, 'robbing you of some of the sickest waves the day had to offer?'"

He touches my elbow lightly, scooting past me into the house. "We've got a little extra time."

"Since when?"

"Since that wet mud coffee was pushed into my

hands this morning. Besides," he says, leaning down and kissing me gently on the cheek, "you've gotta make time for some things. Sometimes the little things are the big ones in life."

I groan, shoving him toward the kitchen. "Go. Do whatever you gotta do, but please no more wisdom. It's too early and you're too cheesy."

"Slow down. Life moves pretty fast. If you don't stop and look around once in—"

"Go!"

I sit at the table blissfully eating my sandwich and watching Lawson move around my mom's kitchen like he belongs there. I wonder if he does. The way he cooks, I think he belongs in any kitchen anywhere. He talks to my mom as he works, showing her what he's doing, suggesting variations. Making her smile. Making her laugh.

She's immediately smitten with him the way all women are and the part that makes me the happiest is that I can tell she's smitten with the *real* him. Not the filler because that's not what he's giving her. He's giving her Lawson. And she is just eating it up.

"My mom is a little in love with you," I tell him an hour later when we're finally on the road.

He chuckles. "She's in love with the sandwich. It makes it hard to see straight."

"Good. She can make one for my dad and he can get all confused too. Maybe let you start coming inside the house."

"I doubt it, but that's okay."

"No it's not."

"Yeah, it really is, Rach." He glances at me out

of the corner of his eye. "I don't want him to like me. It keeps me working for it. It keeps me honest."

"That doesn't make any sense."

"That's because you're not a dude."

"Thank goodness for that," I mutter, taking a sip of my delicious replacement coffee.

"I want you to come over to the house."

I pause, not sure I heard him right. "When?"

"Next Thursday night."

"Why?"

"For dinner."

"With your family?"

"Yeah."

I roll my tongue in my mouth, choosing my next words carefully. "How much of your family."

"All of it," he answers heavily.

"Oh."

He glances at me quickly, gauging my reaction. I'm not giving him much of one.

"Well, not my crazy Aunt Sue," he clarifies. "She's in rehab."

"And not your mom."

"No. She doesn't come to Isla Azul. Her or her new husband."

"What's his name again?"

"Atticus."

"That's a bullshit name."

He snorts. "It's perfect if you're a 1920's barber."

"Is he?"

"That would mean keeping a job. He doesn't have time for that. He's too busy updating his foodie blog."

I wrinkle my nose in disgust. "Yuck."

"Yeah."

Five minutes later and we're pulling into the beach parking lot, a place that's starting to feel like a second home to me. When Lawson puts the car in park I reach for my door handle, but the lock snaps quickly into place.

I look at him, confused. "Am I being taken hostage?"

He shakes his head seriously. "You didn't answer me."

"Why do you want me to have dinner with your family, Lawson?"

"Because I like you and they'll like you too."

"Will I be allowed to talk about it to anyone?"

"No."

"Then, no. I appreciate the invite, but I'd rather not. Not if I have to lie about it."

I've taken him by surprise. Lawson is not accustomed to being told no on anything, and the fact that he's offering me an invite into his home, into his life, is huge. The fact that I'm saying no is even bigger.

It's not that I want to be different or stand out. I'm not telling him no simply so I can say I did. The honest truth is that I do not want to be part of the lie. I wish I didn't know about Aaron being in town because I can't do anything with the knowledge. I can't help Katy, I can't help Aaron, and I definitely can't help Lawson because he's not telling me everything. All I can do is listen, but if he takes me to dinner with his family, if I *see* Aaron, it jumps from being a secret to being a lie. I'll have to lie to the girl who has been like a sister to me my entire life, and that is not something I'm willing to do. Not for any guy. Not even for Lawson Daniel.

"I don't want to ask you to lie," he explains, taken aback by my answer.

"Then don't," I tell him, softening it with, "Please. I really can't lie to Katy and if I have dinner with Aaron I'll have to lie to her eventually. I don't want to do that so please don't put me in that position."

He nods, his eyes locked on the steering wheel. On anything but me. "Yeah, I get that. You're right. I'm sorry."

"Thanks."

He grins crookedly, looking at me sideways with an amused glint in his eyes.

It takes me a second to realize what he thinks is so funny. "Oh, give me a break! It's been nearly two months. You're still on this?"

"I told you, it's fun for me."

"I thought surfing was fun for you. Are you doing that today or did I get up before God to sit in a car with you and shoot the shit?"

"I don't know," he says with a shrug, settling into his seat. "I'm pretty good with this."

"You're not serious."

He abruptly reclines his seat back, laying down. "I'm always serious."

"You absolutely are not."

"Well, I am right now. Lay down. Take a load off."

"Lawson."

He reaches into the back and pulls up a black

baseball hat that he lays over his face. "You got your sandwich," his voice comes out muffled and low. "What are you bitching about?"

"This is for real? We came out here to go to sleep?"

He lifts the hat off one eye. "I came out here to be with you. That's what I'm doing."

I sigh, feeling my heart constrict in my chest. "I never know when you're serious."

"I'm always serious," he repeats, lowering the hat.

He's not kidding. He's taking a nap. Got me up at the crack of dawn to bring me to the beach and take a nap. What the hell?

Less than five minutes later and he's quietly sawing logs under that damn hat. I'm not good at napping, never have been (just ask my mom, she'll tell you all about what a horrible baby I was), so I unlock my door and step outside. Lawson doesn't stir. I look in the window to find him lying there perfectly still and suddenly I realize that something is off. Something I can't believe I didn't notice until right now standing beside his car.

The roof rack is empty. Lawson didn't bring a board with him today.

I scowl at the car, then at him. The car again. The ocean, as though that bipolar bitch can give me any answers, but no one is talking. No one speaks up to explain why Lawson brought me out here today with absolutely no intention of surfing. He's not even wearing his board shorts! I guess it explains why he wasn't concerned at all with hanging in my mom's kitchen for an hour playing

Paula Dean.

I came out here to be with you.

"No," I scold myself, stopping the thought before it starts. It's a dangerous one. It can take me down a path I'll be walking alone. One I'll look up from someday thinking I was on my way to paradise and realize I've trekked down into hell.

You, Rachel Mason, are quickly becoming my favorite person on the planet.

"Dammit."

I head down to the beach. I kick off my shoes and leave them where they fall, sinking into the cool wet sand and heading straight for the surf. It halts me at its edge, whispering over my toes and sifting the sand out from under my feet. I sink lower. I fall deeper, and I'm barely breathing as I stand there.

I've been so afraid all summer, but as I look at the ocean I wonder what it really was I've been scared of. Boston and money, the heat and the ache in my leg – was it all that kept me awake at night? I thought it was, but now I'm not so sure.

Boston is weeks away, the morning is cool and clear, and I'm still shaking scared.

"You lost your shoes."

I turn to find him standing just behind me, my sandals hanging loosely from his fingers. He looks so good. So beautiful and casual, so right in his frayed cargo shorts and his faded T.

It makes me so fucking afraid.

"Take me home, Lawson," I tell him thickly.

His brow falls, darkening his eyes. "Why?"

"Because I can't keep doing this with you."

"Doing what?"

"Spending time with you. Sleeping with you. I thought I could handle letting it be just a fling, but I can't. I…" I breathe in slowly, calming my aching heart. "I didn't know you and I do now and I can't handle it. I can't handle you. You're… goddammit, you're too much. You're so much more than I thought you were and it's too much to walk away from but I have to."

He drops my shoes and stares at me placidly, his chest rising and falling in an unnervingly even rhythm, unreadable emotions flooding his eyes.

"What have I ever done that would make you think this was just a fling for me?"

"Nothing," I whisper, realizing it's true. He never did anything to make me think this wasn't genuine.

Nothing but be Lawson Daniel.

"I spend almost every day with you," he reminds me. "I haven't so much as looked at another girl since the night we hooked up. I told you shit that I've never told anyone. Things I swore I'd never talk about."

"I know. I'm sorry."

"I don't want you to be sorry, Rachel. I want you to be real with me. I want you to look at this, at *us*, and honestly think about it. What do you want from me? 'Cause I'm here," he says, spreading his arms open wide. "I'm asking and I'm giving. This isn't a front and it's not a fling. I'm willing to go the distance with you 'cause I love you."

I stare at him, my face openly shocked. My jaw is on the floor and my head is buzzing with so much static I can't have heard him right.

"What did you say?" I ask slowly.

"I love you," he repeats, not the least bit sorry or ashamed. He drops his arms at his sides, his palms making a smart *smack* against his legs. "And just so there's no more confusion between us, I'll give it to you straight – I'm *in* love with you."

My eyes sting with salt and sweet sorrow. With the fear that's been building and bursting and is now brought to the surface, buoyed by his words and his honest eyes. It rises from the cold depths of the ocean floor and bursts into the air, trembling with life and an unthinkable joy.

"I love you too," I confess, my throat constricting around the words. Hugging them and holding them before letting them go to him. Before giving them up forever. "I'm *in* love with you too."

"Then quit trying to dump me, would you?"

I laugh shakily. "I'll try. I just… I'm scared."

He takes hold of me, pulling me close. "Me too. I've never been in love before."

"Me either."

"So I'm you're first?"

"Looks like it."

"And you're mine."

He pulls back slightly, looking down into my eyes and I want to leave the moment as it is. I want to swim in those perfect pools of green forever, but I know that I can't. I can't keep avoiding everything, hoping it will go away.

"I leave in three weeks," I remind him reluctantly.

"Take me with you."

I chuckle, burying my sadness under the sound.

"There's no surfing in Boston."

"Savages."

"Let's hope not."

Lawson's hold on me tightens. "Don't go," he says seriously.

My heart halts in my chest as he gives life to the want in my blood. "I have to," I protest weakly.

He sighs, pulling me close again until my head is resting on his shoulder and his chin on the top of my head. The ocean plays at our feet, happy and alive, but we stand perfectly still in the midst of it, clinging to each other as the unmistakable ticking of time echoes on the wind. As our moment steadily winds down around us.

"We lived our entire lives within five miles of each other," he mumbles thoughtfully. "We went to the same schools, the same parties. We know all of the same people, so why now? Why did we have to wait until you're leaving to really see each other?"

"Bad timing, I guess."

He snorts unhappily. "Story of my life."

CHAPTER EIGHTEEN

Lawson is competing in the Vans US Open in Huntington Beach the next week. It's a World Qualifying Series event, meaning if he wins, he not only takes home prize money that counts toward his ranking for a bid at the ASP World Tour but he earns points that help him as well. He won the Shoe City Pro down by the pier on this same beach back in January, taking home $6,000 and a thousand points. That sounds like a lot of money but when you take into consideration the fact that the next three qualifying events were in Australia, then Hawaii, Argentina, Tahiti, and Martinique before coming stateside again, it doesn't come out to much. In fact it ends up being too little which is why a lot of great surfers can't make it to the World Tour. They don't have the money to make it to the events, pay for lodging, and entrance fees. And even if you get there, there's no guarantee you'll win a purse. Lawson was at the Oakley Lowers Pro in San Clemente back in April but he didn't win. He barely placed. Bad fog, bad waves.

Bad timing.

"What day does your flight leave?" Katy asks me as we weave through the crowds.

There are tents set up everywhere with vendors,

competitors, and spectators. The place is packed.
It's a madhouse, one I'm not even sure we'll be able
to find Lawson in until he takes to the water but
Katy and I keep trying anyway.

"I don't know yet," I mumble vaguely, half
hoping she can't hear me over the crowd and the
boom of the announcers on the loudspeakers.

"What do you mean you don't know yet?" she
shouts.

"I mean I haven't bought my ticket yet!"

"What happened? I thought you saved up
enough money for one."

"I did."

"So what happened?"

"Nothing."

She pulls on my arm, stopping me in the crowd
and turning me to face her. People bump into us,
pushing past, but I ignore them as she holds me
steady with her serious stare. "You wanna tell me
what your deal is before we get there or are you
going to start keeping secrets from me?"

I cringe, biting back the truth about Aaron. I've
been doing that a lot lately. It feels like lying. It
feels wrong.

"I told him I love him," I tell her quickly and
quietly. "Right after he told me he loves me."

"Holy fucking shit. When?"

"A week ago."

"And you're only telling me now?"

"I've been trying to figure out what it means."

"It means you're in love, dummy."

"Yeah, but what about me leaving?"

"So you love him from Boston," she tells me

like it's obvious. Like it's all so simple. "Long distance relationships aren't doomed if it's the right people. Do you trust him?"

"I do. I trust him completely."

"Then what's the problem?"

"I don't know."

"Well, then that's what it all means. It means you love him, you trust him, and you go to school."

"No," I tell her clearly. "The fact that I don't know is the problem. I don't know what I want to do. I don't know if I want to go and risk it or stay and give us a shot. We're so new it feels dicey flying across the country and putting that kind of distance between us."

She scowls at me. "But that's your life. The NEC is what you've been building to for the last fifteen years. It's your dream. You can't throw it away over a summer romance."

"If it's my dream then why haven't I practiced all summer?"

She takes a half step back, as though I shoved her. "You haven't? You always practice. Every day."

"Not since the accident. I've practiced maybe three times this summer."

"You're kidding me."

I swallow thickly, my nerves jittering in my limbs with a weird electricity as I realize that no, I'm not kidding. I rarely let myself think about it, but it's true. I've barely touched a piano all summer. I've sat on beaches morning, noon, and night. I've spent hours working in a surf shop in Malibu. I've been on a surf board in the ocean that nearly killed me, but I haven't spent more than six hours on a piano bench. I immersed myself in Lawson, got lost in him, and I never took a second to think about the fact that I was using him to hide from myself. To hide from my future.

It doesn't mean I don't genuinely love Lawson. It doesn't mean I don't want with my whole heart to stay here with him. It doesn't even mean I have a better understanding of what it is I need to do in two weeks when I'm supposed to be Boston bound, but it does mean I need to take some time to figure it all out. And I need to do it on my own.

Of course it's then that I spot him. He's in a tent with Wyatt only thirty feet away, his body hidden under a competition jersey but I know it by heart. I know *him* by heart, and the thought of leaving him soon makes me breathless. I feel the way I did on the beach with Katy months ago, saying goodbye and wanting to take every ounce of California summer sun with me that I could. I want to absorb Lawson into my skin – his touch, his smell, his voice, his heart – and know it's with me wherever I go. How can a person leave something so beautiful behind? How can you kiss the coast goodbye and never know if you'll see it again?

"Rachel," Katy says emphatically. It doesn't sound it's the first time she's said it.

I snap my eyes back to hers, coming out of my stupor. "I don't know," I tell her solidly. "I don't know what I'm going to do but I'm going to figure it out."

"When? 'Cause the clock is ticking here."

"I know that. I'll decide soon. Just not here.

Not today."

Katy's eyes soften sadly. "You can't put your life off forever, Rach."

"Yeah, well, neither can you."

I regret it the second I say it. True as it may be, it shouldn't have been said. Definitely not by me.

Her mouth tightens at the edges. "You're talking about Aaron."

"Aren't we always talking about Aaron? Even when you won't say his name, it's who we're talking about. It's who you're thinking about."

"It's not the same thing. Not even close."

"You're right," I concede wholeheartedly. "You're absolutely right, but you of all people have to see where I'm coming from. You have to understand why I'm scared to leave him and Isla Azul behind. If I go away..." I sigh, feeling my eyes sting with harsh tears and truths. "If I go away nothing will be the same when I come back."

Katy laughs. "Are you for real? Of course it'll be the same. Nothing in Isla Azul ever changes."

"That's not true and you know it."

"Okay," she agrees, her smile fading instantly. "You're right. Things changed for me when Aaron left, but what do you expect? You'll go away for a year and come back to find the place deserted? I'm not going anywhere and if the last few years have been any indication, neither is Law."

"Do you promise you and Lawson won't replace me with some skinny rando bitch?"

Katy laughs, pulling me into a tight hug. "I solemnly swear to only hang with familiar fat bitches while you're gone. And I won't like any of them, I promise."

I smile, hugging her hard. "I love you."

"I love you too." She pulls back, looking at me sternly. "But you better figure your shit out. And fast, or I'm going to take drastic action."

"Like what?" I chuckle. "Send another shark after me?"

She swats at me, turning to lead us toward Lawson and Wyatt. "Too soon, you jerk."

"It's been months."

"It could be years. I'll never get it over it. But I'm proud of you for managing it."

"Couldn't have done it without Lawson."

"Yeah," she agrees thoughtfully. "He's a lifesaver."

Lawson laughs when he sees Katy and I, motioning us closer and meeting us halfway. He kisses me immediately, light and sunny, and pulls Katy into a short hug. It surprises all of us, not because the boys don't love Katy like she's their own but because Lawson has kept his distance since his brother disappeared. This show of affection is a testament to how high he flies when he's competing. Or when he's in love.

Wyatt hugs Katy as well, a little too long but I still think it's not long enough. She laughs awkwardly when he finally lets her go but her cheeks are pink. Pinker than the heat can take credit for.

"When are you up?" I ask Lawson.

"Soon." He points to the waves where surfers are already out. "We've been watching the water breaking. Checking out where the biggest waves are coming in."

"He's judged by what maneuvers he does on the wave," Wyatt explains, "and how difficult they are, how powerful, where they're positioned on the wave, but they also consider the size of the wave he surfs."

"So the bigger the wave, the bigger the score?" I ask.

Lawson waves his hand back and forth in a so-so motion. "Kind of. Big or small, it all comes down to how well I ride it."

"But you ride like a god."

He smiles slyly. "That's why I'm gonna win."

"Are there pros here?"

"Yeah. A few," he shrugs, unconcerned.

"And that doesn't worry you?"

"Do you want it to?" Wyatt asks, his tone tight.

Lawson only laughs. "Why would it? They don't control how I surf. I do."

I grin, pointing to his familiar white board. To Layla. "Well, and her."

"And you," he amends, slinging his arm over my shoulder and pulling me close to his side.

We watch more of the competition from under the tent with him, but it's not long before he's up. He kisses me 'for luck' and runs out into the surf with Layla by his side, another guy running into the water not far from him. I wait with a churning stomach for him to find his first wave, the time clock running down on his thirty minutes. That's all the time he has to ride as many waves as he can as perfectly as he can in order to impress the judges and move on to the next heat.

I frown when the other guy finds a wave before him.

"He's already in the quarterfinals," Wyatt tells us, though no one asked. He's watching Lawson intently. He's nervous, I can see it in his stance. "This is the second day of the event and he's already beat just about everybody. It's just him, a few pros, and some other amateurs."

"Do we need to worry about any of the amateurs?" Katy asks.

"Yeah." Wyatt nods to the guy in the water with Lawson. "Adriano Manello. He almost won the Oakley Lowers Pro. Lawson didn't finish the quarterfinals of that one. The guy is good."

"Lawson is better," I reply confidently.

"You've never seen Manello compete."

"I don't have to know Manello. I know Lawson. He'll win."

The echo of the loudspeakers and the theft of the wind makes it almost impossible to understand what they announcers are saying as Lawson finds his first wave. Luckily Wyatt has an app up on his phone that's broadcasting the commentary, bringing it to us with a small delay but way clearer.

"As always Daniel comes out with a big opening turn, throwing tons of spray... Oh! He carved it right in front of Manello!"

Wyatt chuckles, shaking his head.

"Why is that funny?" I ask.

He shrugs. "'Cause Manello's a dick."

I watch patiently as Lawson cuts through the wave, keeping just ahead of the curl and riding high on the break where he snaps his board hard, sending white spray in a brilliant arc up into the air. If it's power they're looking for, they found it. He swings down, kicks back up, and sprays over and over again, changing up his style but always in control. Always riding in the tightest part of the wave.

"...lofty backside air..." the announcers continue. "And he lands it, clean and clear. Looks like a backside snap as this wave is winding down, but tell it to Daniel because he's sticking with it. Milking it for all it's worth with a forehand snap on the right... and he's done. Solid performance by Lawson Daniel. Really the kind of thing we've come to expect from this guy and every year he delivers. Strong competitor giving us aerial maneuvers with almost every turn."

Manello gets ahold of a big wave at the end of the time but he can't hold onto it. He rushes it and flounders inside the whitewater, recovering before he wipes out but emerging from the whitewater with an angry frown on his face.

He was good, but Lawson was flawless and his one hasty mistake might have cost him the heat.

Fans rush the beach as Lawson emerges from the water. I notice quickly that there's an entire camp of fans dedicated to him sitting center beach and it doesn't surprise me. A lot of these surfers are international, coming from every corner of the globe, but Lawson is a local boy. A surfing legend in the area since he was just a kid. A few little boys and a couple of young girls ask him for autographs which he happily signs. Guys his age give him a nod and a fist bump. Girls in nothing but bikinis and a smile want to give him hugs and probably their number. Girls with unblemished bodies and big boobs. Girls who are local.

"You can't kill them with your eyes so stop trying," Katy mutters to me under her breath.

I shake my head, clearing my face. "I wasn't."

"Liar."

"Shut up."

"You trust him, remember?"

"Yeah."

"And he loves you, remember?"

I sigh. "Yeah. I remember."

"Lawson's never been big on the groupies," Wyatt assures me, surprising both Katy and I. I hadn't realized he was listening. "He's got a few stories, but mostly from high school. He really calmed down when Aaron joined the Navy and he got serious about going pro."

I look sideways at Katy, gauging her reaction. She doesn't give one. Her face is stony still, her eyes on the empty water, and I wonder what the hell Wyatt was thinking. I also wonder if he didn't drop that name on purpose, intentionally reminding her he's gone.

Leaving them to deal with each other however they want, I hurry down the beach toward Lawson as he approaches.

"That was amazing!" I gush, throwing my arms open to hug him.

He plants his board and picks me up in his arms, holding me tightly above the sand. "I like this," he tells me as his wet jersey seeps water into my tank top, down to my bikini underneath, and onto my burning skin. "Walking out of the water to find you waiting for me. I could get used to this for sure."

I bury my face in the crook of his neck. He smells like sunscreen and sea salt. Like home.

The thought makes my stomach turn painfully.

"I'm getting used to being here," I tell him quietly.

CHAPTER NINETEEN

Manello falls out, sending Lawson on to the Semi-finals and finally the Final heat where he goes head to head with a pro. Same guy who won the event last year.

It's close, but Lawson beats him. He wins the event, takes the purse, and earns himself ten thousand points toward his bid for the World Tour. According to Wyatt, this win lands him in the top five Men's Qualifying Series ranks.

"How many more of these do you have to win to get in the World Tour?" Katy asks over dinner. "You have to be close, right? You've won two of them."

Lawson has taken us to a burger joint he knows of just north of Huntington Beach. It's small inside but the outdoor area is the draw. It used to be a garage, the west side of the building two huge bay doors that slide up into the ceiling and leave you eating outside no matter where you're sitting. The ingredients are all fresh, all locally grown, and they taste like heaven as we watch the late evening waves glistening gold and yellow across the highway. There's a band setting up, one Lawson knows the bassist for, and he promises they're good. He's ordered us a pitcher, pouring hefty amounts into each of our glasses, so it looks like we're staying for a while.

I'm not complaining.

"The top sixteen go to the World Tour," Lawson explains, "but my problem is that I only compete in local events. I'm not allowed to qualify for the World Tour if I only win in California."

"Why not?"

"It's my home turf. It favors me because I know the waters. I have to win heats in other countries to qualify."

"So where are you going next?"

"Nowhere," Lawson replies simply. "This was the last event in California for the year."

Katy shakes her head. "But you just said that you can't qualify if you've only competed here. Why wouldn't you go somewhere else?"

"Too expensive."

"Didn't you just win a shit-ton of money at this event?"

He smiles. "I wouldn't call it a shit-ton."

"Next event is in two days in Chile," I tell Katy, reading off the schedule I've pulled up on my phone. "But that's a thousand point event. Barely worth getting out of bed for let alone getting on a plane. There's two events in September in Portugal. Both ten thousand points apiece." I look up at Lawson, shrugging. "That'd be worth it, right?"

He's watching me with a mix of admiration and amusement. "You're getting the hang of this, aren't you?"

I smile. "I like watching you win."

"I'll do it more often."

"You'll have to if you want to stay in the top sixteen. Portugal next month is your best bet." I plop my phone down next to him on the black mesh table. "Better book your flight now. Trust me, last minute tickets are expensive."

He doesn't reach for my phone. He watches me carefully, his eyes guarded in a way I haven't seen in weeks. "You've been pricing tickets lately?"

"I've been staying informed," I answer carefully.

His eyes linger on mine before dropping to my phone, his head bobbing in a slow nod. "I think I'll pass on Portugal this year."

"Why?" Katy demands incredulously. "You're on a roll. You're in the top tier."

"Bad timing," Lawson answers coolly.

He kicks back his beer and sets his pint glass down firmly, the foam slowly easing down the sides and settling in the bottom of the glass. He reaches over with his now free hand and lays it on my knee. His fingers caress my skin absently, his eyes on the water, and I wish we were alone so I could talk to him. So I could ask him what he's thinking, but part of me is scared to know. I'm not ready to have this conversation yet and I know Katy is right, I know time is running out, but I want to linger here just a minute more. I want to be here with him as much as I can, let him celebrate and enjoy this day because he deserves it. He deserves to be happy.

Lawson wasn't wrong – the band is good. After just three songs I understand why he likes them. They're a Sublime cover band, Lawson's favorite. The four of us finish our burgers, Wyatt and I finish the pitcher of beer, and we watch the sun start to set on the water.

Two hours later and another pitcher split between Wyatt and I and we're ready to head home.

"Hey, Katy," Lawson calls to her when we head out to the parking lot. "You mind if we switch passengers?"

She shrugs. "Sure. Wyatt, you're with me, buddy."

He cringes at the name, but he happily climbs inside her car, tripping once on the way in. He's buzzed and so am I. Katy and Lawson each had one beer from the pitcher at the start of the night but nothing for the last couple hours. Wyatt and I however have probably had too much. I'm all smiles and hands up and down Lawson's arm that might be holding me vertical more than I realize. He leads me toward his shining black car, Layla lovingly strapped to the roof, and I run my hand along her surface as I step toward the passenger door.

"I'm glad you and her are back together," I tell Lawson happily.

He smiles, unlocking the car. "Yeah, me too."

"Did you miss her?"

"Yeah."

"You surfed on other boards but you always wanted her back, didn't you?"

"Yup."

He holds my door open for me, waiting patiently. I don't get in the car. I look up into his handsome face and I feel myself start to crumble inside. His face falls to worry when he sees it.

"If she'd needed more time," I whisper softly, "would you have given it to her?"

"You mean would I have waited for her?" he asks seriously, his voice so lovely and deep.

"Yeah."

"Yes. I would have waited for as long as she needed."

"But you'd still surf. You'd still use other boards."

"Rachel," he begins.

I take a shuddering breath and race forward over his words. "Even if you did, you'd still love her, wouldn't you? Layla. You might take another board out on the waves but you'd always love her."

"Yeah, Rach." He uses both hands to smooth my hair away from my face, out of the wind to where he can see my eyes. He holds my head in his hands steadily. "I would wait and I would always love her."

I stand on my toes and kiss him, tears in my eyes that I don't totally understand. I'm a mess of emotions and beer and confusion. I'm so lost and so torn that even the taste of his lips doesn't set me straight. The feel of his hands on my skin, his chest under my palms and the perfect beat of his heart isn't enough. It spins me out further, buries me down deeper, and I can't see and I can't breathe and I absolutely cannot think.

I fall back to the flat of my feet and force a shaky laugh. "I'm drunk," I tell him apologetically.

He grins faintly, but it doesn't look convincing. It doesn't reach is eyes. "A little bit, yeah."

"Will you take me home? I need to get to

sleep."

"Yeah, of course."

It takes over two hours to drive home from Huntington Beach. We're quiet almost the entire way. I try to talk to Lawson about his competition and the other people who were there, the pros and the amateurs he's grown up with, but eventually he falls silent and I fall asleep. I barely wake up enough for him to walk me to my door. He assures me he can see Katy's car in her driveway next door, telling me she made it home safe, and he offers to help me to bed. It's late, though, and I can only imagine the wrath my dad would show us if he saw Lawson Daniel leaving my bedroom at this time of night.

He kisses me goodbye sweetly, waiting until he hears me lock the door to go back to his car. I listen as he starts it up and drives away. I wait until I can't hear the engine anymore. Until the feel of his lips on mine fades. I stand there in the dark in the living room waiting for him to leave my senses, to feel what that's like and imagine it lasting not just a day but a week and a month. A year.

I stand there in the dark.

And I cry.

CHAPTER TWENTY

"Wake up!"

A painful snap hits the end of my nose, jolting me awake. I swat wildly, connecting with something soft and hard at the same time. Something that shouts and hits me back.

"Crap!"

My eyesight is blurry with sleep but I make out the outline of Katy standing next to my bed. She's holding her right breast and glaring at me.

"You hit me in the boob, you bitch," she hisses.

I touch my nose, the sting still strong. "You flicked me in the face. You get what you give."

"I was trying to wake you up."

"Why? Why would you wake a person up that way?"

"Because you refused to wake up when I yelled at you!"

"Well I'm awake now so stop yelling at me!"

She sags, collapsing on my bed and across my legs. "Okay," she replies glumly.

I try to sit up but she has me pinned. "What's the matter?"

"I had a weird night."

"After you left Huntington Beach?"

"Yeah."

"What happened?"

She rolls dramatically onto her back, her hair splaying out over my comforter and her body freeing my legs from her weight. "Wyatt kissed me."

"Seriously?"

"Yes. Very seriously."

I smile, sitting up excitedly and shaking her arm. "That's good news, right? He's a great guy and he's had a thing for you forever."

"I know."

"Did you kiss him back?"

"Yeah. A lot."

"How much is a lot?"

"For like an hour."

I giggle happily, earning a glare from her.

"This isn't a good thing," she warns me.

"Why not? The kiss couldn't have been bad if you did for a solid hour."

"Probably longer, and no. It wasn't bad. It was actually really, really great. I haven't kissed a guy in over a year and when he did it I just... I lost my mind. I mounted him, Rach."

"Whoa."

"Yeah. I straddled him in his seat and I attacked him."

"And it was good?"

"It was so good. That boy knows how to kiss."

"Did he try anything?"

She throws her arm over her eyes, shaking her head. "No."

"Did you want him to?"

"No."

"So why are you treating this like it's a bad thing?"

"Because he's a good guy! Good guys are the worst."

I laugh, pulling her arm off her face. "That's not true and you know it. They're the best. You're just scared to like him."

She shakes her head. "That's not it."

"Then what's the problem?"

"I feel guilty. Like I cheated on Aaron."

I reach out and flick the end of her nose hard.

She shrieks, sitting up and scurrying away from me to the end of the bed. "What the hell?!"

"No," I scold her sternly.

"Are you talking to me like I'm a dog?"

"Yes. You're a bad girl! Stop it!"

"But I feel gui—"

"Stop it!"

She throws a pillow at me. "You stop it."

I swat the pillow away, settling in seriously. "You can't feel guilty about Aaron, Katy. It's over."

"You don't know that. No one knows that because he's not here. Who knows where he is?"

I shake my head, shrugging helplessly and avoiding her eyes.

"Lawson knows, doesn't he?" she asks quietly.

The fact that she's asking doesn't bother me. She's shown a lot of restraint in the last two months. She's given me a lot of time for Lawson and I to be just that – Lawson and I. She's never asked me to find out where Aaron is and that couldn't have been easy for her. But with Wyatt's kiss and her guilt and her never ending longing for a man who is dead set on disappearing, it was inevitable that this moment would come.

And I will not lie to her.

"Yeah, he does," I tell her hesitantly.

"Do *you* know where he is?"

"Yeah. I do."

She takes in a quick, shaking breath. "And you didn't tell me?"

I feel sick inside with the secret I've kept, and when I meet her eyes I hope she can see that. I hope she can forgive me. "I swore I wouldn't."

"Where is he, Rach? Is he alive?"

"Yes."

"Where?"

"He's here. He's in Isla Azul."

She's shocked into silence. Her eyes blink several times but it's the only reaction I see. Then she laughs.

"Are you fucking with me?" she asks, smiling.

"No. He's really here. He's at his parent's house."

She laughs again, standing up and turning in a circle, not sure what to do with herself. "That is... oh my God. Rachel, that is the best news!"

"No, it's not," I tell her urgently, standing to face her. "It's really not. He's been here for months. Something happened in the military and he's back now and he doesn't want people to know."

Her smile disappears. "What happened to him?"

"I don't know. Lawson wouldn't tell me."

She goes to dresser, opens my underwear drawer, and flings a piece of white fabric at my face. "Put a bra on," she demands. "We're going over there."

"Katy, we can't."

"Aaron Daniel is in Isla Azul." She points out the window. "He's less than five miles away and you think there's anything on this earth that's going to stop me from going over there and seeing him?"

"He doesn't want anyone to see him."

"Well then he should have gone to the moon! He owes me answers and I'm going to get the goddammit!"

She bursts from my room and heads for the front door.

I hurriedly throw on my bra and follow her out of the house.

She's twitchy on the drive over. I don't bother trying to talk her out of it because this is obviously happening. She's right – nothing on this earth could stop her from going to him. Even if it is to tear him a new one.

Lawson's car is in the driveway when we pull up. I'm surprised by that. It's after eight in the morning. He should be at the beach right now. Part of me wishes he was because when he sees us here, he won't be happy.

Katy has slammed her car door and made a dash for the front of the house before I can even get out. She's ringing the doorbell over and over as I slowly go to join her.

"Come on, come on," she mutters impatiently, looking up at the second story of the house for signs of life.

There's nothing.

"Maybe they're not home," I suggest halfheartedly.

She snorts. "He obviously doesn't get out much or someone would have known he was here." She pounds on the door with her fist, giving up on the doorbell. "Aaron Daniel, I know you're in there! I know you see me out here! Come answer this door and face me like a man! You owe me that much!"

The door swings open, filling instantly with an angry Lawson. He looks from Katy to me, his face darkening when he spots me.

"You told her," he accuses angrily.

I nod slowly. "I said I wouldn't lie to her. She asked me so I told her."

"Where is he?" Katy demands of Lawson. "He's inside, I know he is."

He holds the door halfway closed. "He won't want to see you, Katy. He doesn't want to see anyone."

"Not okay. This is happening. Rachel says he's been here for months. In all that time he couldn't have called me? He couldn't have sent a letter telling me he was alive? I've been waiting for him for almost a year, Lawson! One day he's sending me emails telling me how much he loves me and that he can't wait to see me again, and the next he drops off the face of the earth without a word! Who does that to a girl?!"

"Stop shouting."

"I will not!"

"She has every right to."

The three of us all freeze at the sound of a deep voice behind Lawson. He turns in surprise and I catch a shadowy glimpse of a man in the entryway. He's not as tall as I remember Aaron being. His body is hunched slightly, his head hanging low.

"Let her in, Law," Aaron tells him quietly.

"Are you sure, man?" he asks his brother.

"Yeah. But just her. I'll meet her in the basement. And... will you warn her?"

"Yeah."

Aaron's shadow vanishes deep inside the house. Lawson waits until he's gone entirely before turning back to Katy and I. His face is tired and worn.

"You can go in, Katy. Go down the hall to the door on the right."

"I remember where the basement is, Lawson."

"Okay." He steps onto the porch close to her, speaking quietly. "But watch your reaction when you see him. He's not the same as he used to be and he's sensitive about it. Try not to freak out."

Katy's face crumbles. "What happened to him?"

"You know he was a Navy medic working with the Marines?"

"Yeah."

"He was working on a guy who'd been shot and a grenade was thrown at them. He didn't hesitate. He laid on top of the guy and took the hit. He lost most of his left arm and part of his face. He's lucky to be alive."

"Oh my God," I breathe.

Lawson glances at me sparingly before turning back to Katy. "Remember, don't freak out. Don't even ask about it. He doesn't like to talk about it.

He actually tries really hard to act like it never happened. That's why no one in town knows he's here."

"I can't talk to him about why he's been gone?"

"Ask him why he never told you it was over. That's what you want to know, isn't it?"

"Yeah."

"Then that's what you should ask him. It sounds like he might answer you."

Katy goes to step around him to the house, but Lawson reaches out and takes hold of her arm.

"No more yelling," he tells her severely. "No more banging on doors. He has a hard time with loud noises."

"I won't, I promise. I'm sorry."

Lawson nods, releasing her arm.

Katy goes slowly and silently into the house. Lawson pulls the door shut quietly behind her, leaving us alone on the porch.

"It wasn't your secret to tell," he reminds me angrily.

I sigh, ready for his wrath. "Yeah, well it wasn't yours either. It was his and you told it to me just as much as I told it to Katy."

He clenches his jaw angrily before releasing a harsh breath through his nose. "I guess you're right. This still should have happened on his terms though."

"What about her terms? She's lived with the doubt and heartbreak for almost a year when all it would have taken from him is a note. One text saying it's over. She could have moved on."

"He couldn't do it because *he* can't move on,"

Lawson argues. "He sits in that basement and he pretends it never happened. I'm the only person he talks to half the time and if I left he would probably lock the door to the basement and die down there. He won't talk about it, he won't get therapy like he's supposed to. He could have plastic surgery to repair a lot of the damage to his face but he won't because he won't look in the mirror. He broke every one of them on the ground floor when he came back."

"I'm sorry."

"It's not your—"He stops himself, calming his anger before it can run away with him and I realize that he's not angry with me or Katy. He's angry with Aaron. With what this secret has been doing to his family. To his life. "This is a bad idea, letting her in there."

"No it's not. He needs it as much as she does. He's put his life on pause and it can't stay that way forever. He can't keep *you* that way forever."

"I'm not on pause."

"Wake up, Lawson," I laugh incredulously. "We're all on pause. Katy waiting for him, you sticking around for him, me stalling on the NEC."

"What are you talking about? You've been gunning to get out of here. You're not on pause. You're on fast forward."

I take a breath, fearing what I'm going to say next. I've never put it words before. Never said it out loud or even let the thought fully form in my head, but if I can confess it to anyone, it's Lawson.

"When that shark bit me I was relieved."

He stares at me blankly. "What?"

"Not the moment he bit me, but when I woke up in the hospital. I was relieved I still had my leg but then even more than that I was relieved I missed my flight to Boston." I swallow thickly, my breath feeling shallow. "I didn't know how long it would take to recover. I hoped it was too long. I was hoping I'd miss the start of school and I'd have an excuse to put it off for another year."

"You spent the first part of the summer searching for a job to get you on a plane."

"Because I knew I was supposed to. It was what everyone expected. Not once did anyone say I should hold off because of the accident so I never told anyone I wanted to, but I did. I do. I don't want to go. I don't want to leave California. I don't want to go to the NEC and find out I'm not as good as I think I am."

He balks at me. "You're incredible. You know that."

"I'm incredible here, but am I incredible in Boston?"

"I don't know."

"Neither do I and that's killing me."

His chest rises and falls in a heavy, labored rhythm. "But you're still going, aren't you?"

"I have to."

"Fuck," he grunts, turning his back on me.

"You know I have to!"

He shakes his head, not responding.

"I have to know," I press. "I'm terrified to leave this town and I need to know why. I have to see what's out there, outside Isla Azul. We've lived our whole lives here and neither of us exactly loves it. What if it's better out there? What if there's something better?"

"Some*one* better?" he asks, his voice hard.

"No. There's no one in the world better than you. But I'm afraid to leave so I have to go. I have to own my fear or it will own me. You taught me that."

His shoulders shake with a quiet chuckle. "Screwed myself on that one, didn't I?"

"Will you look at me, please?"

He turns to face me, his hand brushing quickly under his nose and his eyes avoiding mine. That hurts. It hurts because I'm hurting him, something I never wanted to do.

"I'll be back in nine months," I promise him.

"You want me to wait for you?"

"If you love me is that such a horrible thing to ask?"

"No." He looks up at me then, his face solid. Resolved. "I'd do it. I'd do it in a second if you asked me to, but you won't, will you?"

I pinch my lips together between my teeth, shaking my head.

"Why not, Rachel?"

"I'm pretty sure you know why."

"Say it."

"Because if I'm going to give this a real shot I can't know you're waiting for me on the other side of it. I have to go with no strings. No attachments."

He lets his head fall back, his eyes on the sky. "I'm losing you. Turns out I never even had you and now I'm losing you."

"*You have me*," I tell him fervently. "Lawson,

you have to know that. You have me, all of me. But if I tell myself I'm definitely coming back to Isla then I'm not giving Boston a fair chance. I may as well not go."

He brings his eyes back to mine. "So don't."

"You don't mean that."

"You give me too much credit. I think I do."

"You would want me to stay?"

"If I'm being totally selfish, yeah. I want you to stay. I've never been in love before. Rach. It feels good. Everything feels right with you. And if you go, if you take that with you – Fuck," he curses again, his eyes squinting against the sun. Against everything. "It'll hurt, won't it?"

I close the distance between us, taking his hands in mine. He lets me. He pulls me in close until our bodies are almost touching. Until he can lower his face to rest his forehead against mine.

"I don't want to hurt you," I whisper tremulously.

"But you have to go."

I nod my head, moving his with it until he's nodding too. "I can't live and die here never having given the world a chance. I want to know if I have the talent to be more than this. More than me."

His thumb runs gently over the back of my hand. "You're perfect the way you are."

"If I go there and find out that's true, I'll come back."

He doesn't say anything to that. Just keeps running his thumb along my skin until finally I pull back. I look up into his green eyes so full of so many things no one ever thought him capable of.

Fear and longing. Love. But it's there and it's real and earnest, and it breaks my heart because I knew. I saw him, I heard him. I knew who he was underneath everything we all put on him. I knew he was great. I knew I would love him.

And part of me always knew I would leave him.

CHAPTER TWENTY-ONE

A week goes by without seeing Lawson.

The last time I saw him was at his house with Katy. I waited there with him for her to come out of his house, and when she did, eyes puffy and red from crying, he squeezed my hand, avoided my eyes, and hurried inside.

I drove Katy's car and let her cry quietly the entire way home. I didn't ask and she didn't tell. She wasn't ready yet, but when I hugged her goodbye in her driveway I promised I would be there when she was. I told her to call me day or night to talk. She forced a smile, nodded her head, and then she too hurried inside, leaving me alone on the lawn.

That night I bought my plane ticket to Boston.

I drive myself down to Ambrose Surf the next morning. It's my last day but Lawson doesn't show up early with a brown bag of delicious and I don't call or text him to ask why. It's a stupid question.

I finish out the day, thank Don for the opportunity, and almost cry when he hands me a bonus and tells me I have a job waiting there if I ever want one. I tell him I'll remember that. Then I go to my car, open the envelope, and nearly piss myself when I see how much my bonus is. Five hundred dollars.

"Holy crow," I whisper to the money.

That's more than my plane ticket cost. That's more than enough for a return ticket if I want one.

I close the envelope, closing my eyes as well and breathing deeply. It's a dangerous thing having a way out. I wonder if I should go inside and try to give it back to him. He'd never take it, though, and there's no one I can leave the money with that wouldn't give it to me if I asked for it desperately enough. I'll have to take care of it myself. I have to be strong on my own.

As I'm winding my way up the Pacific Coast Highway, my windows down and my music blasting, I hear the faint ring of my phone in my purse. I think about ignoring it but at the last second I check the display.

Lawson

I fumble to quickly answer it, roll up my windows, and silence my music all at once, all while trying not to crash. It's tricky.

"Hello?" I answer on the last possible ring.

"Hey, Rach."

I smile when I hear him say my name. "Hi. How are you doing?"

"I'm okay," he answers, sounding tired. "I'm in L.A. so you know, not a great day."

"What are you doing in L.A.?"

"I'm at my mom's place. I brought Aaron down late last night. I haven't slept all day."

"God, Lawson, I'm sorry. Is he okay? What happened?"

"He's—yeah, I don't know how he is. He's

shaken up. He's been different since Katy came by. He's finally agreed to see a therapist and start talking about it. Maybe even a plastic surgeon. It's scary though. He's weird right now. Really jumpy. We have to have all of the curtains closed and he won't go anywhere during the day. He'll only travel at night so we had to make a special appointment tonight with the therapist after dark."

"And you're gonna take him?"

"He won't go anywhere without me," Lawson groans. "And I can't go anywhere without him. I told him I had to take a piss, that's the only way I can talk to you right now. I'm locked up in the bathroom like a fugitive."

I frown, my heart aching for him. "You're a good brother."

"I'm a tired brother. I need to sleep but he won't let me. He wants me to keep talking to him."

"About what?"

"Sports. Baseball and basketball. No surfing. It's my nightmare."

"I wish I could help."

"It helps just to hear your voice."

I smile. "You're sappy when you're tired."

"I'm horny when I'm tired too. Say something dirty."

"Truck stop bathroom floors," I whisper breathily.

He chuckles. "You're playing but the voice is doing it for me. Say something else."

"Porn store viewing rooms."

"Nasty girl."

"Spittoons," I moan.

He laughs and it sounds more solid than his voice has since we started talking. "Man, I love you."

"I love you too, Lawson," I tell him in my non-sex phone operator voice. "How long are you going to be in L.A. do you think?"

He hesitates and I immediately know it's bad news. "The month at least."

"Oh."

"Did you buy a plane ticket?" he asks tightly.

"I did. I fly out a week from tomorrow. My last night will be Thursday."

"Shit," he curses angrily. "We've set up appointments with this therapist for the whole month. His second one is Thursday night."

"It's fine."

"I'm sorry."

"It's okay. You've got bigger stuff on your mind."

"It's only an hour and a half drive. Maybe I can get him to let me out of his sight by then and come up after I bring him home from therapy."

"Lawson, that's a lot of maybes and you're going to be exhausted. You have so much on your plate right now, you don't need this too."

"No, but I need you."

I fight the urge to close my eyes. To cry. To turn my car to the east and drive to L.A. to see him just for a second. But he's with his brother and Aaron has made it very clear he doesn't want anyone to see him, even strangers, so I stay the course.

"So sappy," I joke lightly.

"So horny," he replies comically.

"Good thing you're in a bathroom."

"Good thing I have a good memory. Send me a picture, would you?"

"No," I laugh. "Not a chance."

"Not a dirty one. One of your face. I just realized I don't have any."

I smile affectionately. "I will. When I get home I will. Do the same for me?"

"The second I'm not in a bathroom I will."

"Good."

There's a muffled shuffle of the phone on material, footsteps and a hesitant knock.

"Coming," I hear Lawson call softly. More shuffling and his voice comes back at full volume. "Sorry, Rach, but I gotta go. I've been in here a while and Atticus says he's looking for me."

"Go. Do what you need to do and try to get some sleep."

"I will. Send me that picture."

"You too. I love you."

"I love you."

I hang up feeling drained and sad. I keep the windows up and my music muted the rest of the drive home. Before I get there I have an idea, though. I pull off on a familiar old road that winds up the hill. That heads to the bluff. I get out of the car with my phone and pull my hair out of its tie, letting it fly long and wild in the wind. Putting my back to the ocean I smile at the camera. I take a picture of me and the sea and I send it to Lawson.

As I'm getting back in the car my phone beeps once. It's a picture from Lawson. It's him on a couch in a dark room, his tan skin looking impossibly brown and his green eyes half closed with sleep. But he's smiling. He's content and beautiful and all of the things I want to remember about him when I'm gone. His kindness. His calm. His sappy, horny heart.

***

I hear from Lawson every day, but we never say goodbye. Not even at the end of phone conversations. Not even for a second. As we get closer and closer to Thursday I start to get anxious. There are things I want to say to him. Promises I want to make and ones I want to ask of him, but I can't. I have to go into this the way I told him I would – unattached. No strings.

Easier said than done.

Katy comes by for dinner on Thursday night to eat with my parents and I, but she still isn't ready to talk about what happened with Aaron. She looks solid though. Not happy but steady. It takes a load off my shoulders to see her that way.

Wyatt sends me a text saying good luck and goodbye. Baker messages me telling me the same. And yet perfect silence from Lawson.

"Do you want to stay up late?" Mom asks with a small smile when Katy leaves. "Watch a movie? Eat junk food until we pass out on the couch?"

I grin, shaking my head. "No. My flight leaves early and I don't want to be sleep deprived all day traveling. Thanks, though."

"Okay. We'll all get to bed then. See you in the

morning."

I hug her loosely, refusing to let her make this moment a thing because tomorrow it will all happen again. I can't do this multiple times. I'm barely able to do it once.

Dad goes to bed with a quick wave and a hollered 'goodnight'. I'll get a hug out of him in the morning before Mom takes me to the airport. That's about it, but that's all I expect and all I want 'cause that's just how Dad is.

I go to bed with my window open so I can smell the ocean and breathe the air, but I don't let myself think of it as the last time because it's not. I'll be back here to Isla Azul. Maybe not for a long time, and maybe not to stay forever, but I will be back. Just because tomorrow is the start of something new it doesn't mean it's the end of something old. My life is not one or the other, it's what I make it. It's who I am and California is a part of me. It's under my skin, it's in my blood, and I'll always come back for it.

I'll always love it.

***

My phone beeps loudly in the darkness. I groan, fumbling blindly for it to turn off the alarm. I hate getting up early. It feels like I just fell asleep.

My hand connects with the thin rectangle and I open an eye to swipe it to sleep, but it's then I realize it's silent. It only beeped once, not with the alarm but with a message. At two in the friggin' morning.

knock knock

My vision goes weird around the edges, flaring and darkening instantly as my blood flies through my body. I drop my phone on the bed and make a mad dash through the dark house, heading for the front door. When I swing it open I'm not disappointed.

In the wan moonlight stands Lawson. He's in shorts and an STP T-shirt with a small hole just below the collar. I can see his skin through it, smooth and tan. Warm in the way that makes me sweat just looking at him. His green eyes are too dark to see but I can feel them on me. Enveloping me.

He doesn't say a word and I don't ask any questions as he backs me slowly into the house. He closes the door softly behind him and stalks me through the living. Through the hall. To my bedroom where he again closes the door. Where he deftly lifts his shirt up over his head, shuffles effortlessly out of his shorts, and stands in front of me nearly naked with no inhibition and no question of why he's here.

I pull my tank top off, letting my long hair fall out of it over my shoulders. He reaches out and gently pushes it aside, exposing my body to him. He takes it in like he's memorizing it and I imagine that's exactly what he's doing. It's what I'm doing as I stare at him, my mouth open slightly to pass my thin breaths across my lips. I feel like I'm struggling for air. Like I can't get enough of it or him or the night.

Lawson kneels slowly in front of me as he pulls

my shorts down to lie in a pool on the floor. His hands rise slowly over my legs, following the contours, tracing the muscles and the curves. He pauses on my right thigh where the scars pock the tan surface, white and reluctant to brown. He touches them with his fingers. He kisses them with his lips. Every last one of them, all the way around my leg in tender drops of worship until I'm faint. Until my hands are on his shoulders, worried I'll collapse.

And when his mouth moves higher, I fall apart completely.

Lawson pushes me back, tumbles me to my bed, and then he stretches his body out over mine. He doesn't flinch away from staring down into my eyes and he doesn't hide anything in his. I find the whole of the world in their depths. The ocean and the sky, the air over my head and the earth under my feet. The blood in my veins and the beat of my heart. Love and devotion. Loss and surrender.

I find Lawson there.

I find my first love, my last kiss, my life in slow motion, and I slip beneath the surface to give it all back. I give him my breath and my body, pulling him close, so close it hurts, and the moon is still on his skin, shifting the tide. Moving us in and out in time with its breath. I'm dizzy and breaking apart, drifting higher and higher into the night sky in tiny incandescent pieces that burn brighter than stars. That shine down on the world, reflect back on the water in his eyes, in the depths of his soul, until we're infinite.

Until we're everything.

CHAPTER TWENTY-TWO

In the morning I'm alone.

I stayed awake with him all night, silent and star-struck until we could feel the sun coming. We could hear it on the horizon and I needed him gone before this day dawned. I needed it the way I needed his body last night. His kiss, his unrelenting heat, but it couldn't live beyond last night. Last night was love and today is goodbye, and there's no room for both in my body right now. If I looked at him in the daylight on today of all days, I wouldn't get on that plane. And I have to, have to, have to get on that airplane.

I have to know what I'm so afraid of.

My dad does exactly as I expected – quick hug, firm but brief, and a guttural goodbye. He's sad and I know it but we don't talk about it and I don't ask him for more than that. That's what he has and that's what I get, and that's just fine.

Mom cries when I go to my gate and leave her at security. I try not to cry too but I do. I'm a weepy, weak baby leaving her mommy and I can hardly handle it. I'm a grown woman, twenty-one years old, and I'm scared because I've never flown by myself. It feels pathetic but it's real.

I'm afraid.

Six hours later and I'm terrified. LAX is a big airport. It's huge, but it's familiar. I've been there countless times dropping people off and picking them up. I know the layout. I know the drill. Logan International is a completely different beast and I feel overwhelmed just standing in it. I'm panicking, doubting myself before I've even collected my luggage, and I know I need to do something quick before I use that bonus to buy a plane ticket back home.

I pull out my phone, feeling tears sting my eyes for the second time today, and realize there's only one person I can call to get me through this.

"Hey, how was your flight?" Katy answers immediately.

The happy sound of her voice, light and excited, messes with my insides. I nearly double over with the pain in my stomach. "I've made a mistake," I tell her tremulously.

She's immediately all business. "What happened?"

"I hate it here."

"How long have you been there? Five minutes?"

"Ten."

"Rachel," she sighs heavily.

I sit down in an uncomfortable gray plastic seat, pulling my rolling bag close so I can lay my forehead against it and hide my watery eyes. "I need to come back home."

"You need to give this thing a shot. You're not even trying."

"I never wanted to do this."

"Yeah, you did. You always wanted to do this. You just wanted it to be easy, but guess what? If getting out of Isla Azul was easy everyone would do it. You and Lawson—"

"Please don't say his name," I burst out, goosebumps erupting over my skin. "I can't hear his name or I seriously will come home right now. You can't talk to me about him or tell me what he's doing, okay? I can't know or I'll never give this a fair shot."

"You're not giving it a fair shot now!"

"I called you instead of him, didn't I?! Now talk me out of it."

"I was trying to."

"Try again, without using his name."

She pauses, debating before quietly pointing out, "You realize our roles are reversed now, right? I can say Aaron's name without falling apart but you can't say... somebody else's name."

"The Daniel boys are cursed," I moan.

"Ain't that the truth."

"Can I ask how you're doing with that yet? You never told me what you guys talked about."

"Oh, well, shit," she groans. "We talked about everything. He told me the entire plot line to Game of Thrones so far. It's messy."

"So I've heard."

"He told me he was sorry."

I stare at the ugly carpet on the floor, wide eyed. "That's huge."

"Yeah. It was nice to hear. I told him I was sorry too."

"For what?"

"For all the times I thought the worst about him. I assumed he'd found someone new and just forgot about me. I thought he was an asshole."

"And now you don't think he is?"

"No," she answers gently. "Now I think he's hurt. Really badly hurt in a million ways and I can't fix a single one of them. And he doesn't want me to try."

"So... that's it then?"

"That's it," she confirms matter-of-factly.

"Wow."

"Yeah. But it's good 'cause now I know. It's over. He made it clear he isn't the same guy I fell in love with. He doesn't want me to try to get to know him again. He doesn't want anyone from town to come near him. So I won't. It's all I can do for him so I'll do it."

"You gonna be okay?"

"Eventually. How about you?"

I sigh, sitting back in my seat with dry eyes. "I don't know."

"What I was going to say before you bit my head off about the unspeakable name was that you and him are special. The entire town knows it and we take pride in your talents. That's why we want you to take them out to the world. Not because we're sick of your face and we want you gone, but because you take us with you somewhere we can't go. If La—if he wins a surfing tournament in Mexico, that's a win for Isla Azul too and the big bad world can suck it for looking down on our small town. If you join the Boston Orchestra or whatever they have there, *we* get to do it too. We're in concert halls surrounded by diamonds and instruments worth more than a car because you took us there. You guys have to bring the world to us because we're not getting out."

"You could."

"Not like you can. Not with a bang."

"I don't think I'm really bangin' right now," I remind her unhappily. "I feel more like a mouse fart."

"Ew."

"Yep."

"Get your ass out of that airport," she tells me sternly. "Go bang that goddamn drum all up and down the streets of Boston. And take me with you when you do it."

I stand up, taking hold of the handle of my suitcase with a sweaty palm. "Can I call you every day?"

"Yes. Every single day. But only if you've done something that day. If you hide in your apartment and whine, I'll hang up on you."

"No, you won't," I chuckle.

"Try me."

"I'll talk to you tomorrow."

"Okay. Be brave, Sharmalade."

"Ugh," I grunt in annoyance. "Freakin' Wyatt."

"He's infectious."

"Like herpes?"

"Like a good herpes. Like a candy coated herpes."

I laugh, the feeling sending bubbles through my body that make me feel instantly lighter. Alive like whitewater.

"You're gross."

"We both are."

"I'll talk to you later?" I ask hopefully.

"After you've accomplished something. Something outside your house."

I roll my bag down the concourse, heading for the exit with my heart in my throat. "I'll see what I can do."

***

My roommates names are Molly, Heather, and Asper. Yeah. Asper. He plays the cello, wears cardigans, thick black glasses, eats only organic, and is a total pain in the ass. He's also a comfort. He reminds me of home, of all the pretentious, douche hipsters Katy and I used to make fun of whenever we'd go to L.A. Heather and Molly are pretty cool if not a little reserved and quiet. They're both pretty serious. They don't much like modern music or movies. They're big readers, mostly titles I've never heard of. But I did see a worn copy of Twilight on the coffee table one morning. No idea who it belonged to but I sure as shit know it wasn't mine.

Asper and I are the only ones who watch TV, but even there I can't find common ground with him. He's mostly into cooking shows and Tiny House Hunting. Urban bee keeping and being a total chode. So I keep to myself a lot but I make a point of going outside the apartment every day. I take walks, I explore the campus. I learn the public transportation system and go more than a block from my front door. Boston is a beautiful old city with a million things to see and explore. It's not hard to stay busy. It's not hard to keep my mind off things.

Not until I go to sleep. That's when I start to miss everything. That's when the cool of the air conditioner pisses me off and I miss the stifling heat of my parent's house. I miss the sound of my dad getting up in the morning, the smell of coffee wafting down the hall. I miss my mom making breakfast before going to work and yelling at me to remember to do the dishes before she got home. Katy next door. Lawson's car in the driveway. The salt on the air.

Sometimes I feel weak. I turn on my phone and I lay it on the pillow where I can see it. Where I can see Lawson's face on the screen, half asleep and happy, and I hope that's how he looks in that moment. I hope it's how he feels. And it's selfish and I know it, but I hope he's missing me as much as I'm missing him.

He's keeping quiet – not texting or calling. He's letting me have what I asked for. He's letting me have this chance to figure me out when it's just me. All alone.

It's what I wanted, right?

Right?

Mom and Katy are keeping mum about him too. I have no idea what he's doing, how his brother is doing, and part of me feels bad about that. I feel like I should ask. Like I should call him and be there for him if he needs it because what if he does? What if I could help him through this? But I never call because I think it would just confuse things. For both of us.

Suddenly Heather plops down next to me on the couch, the cushions warn and faded. Scratchy on my legs where my capris leave them bare.

"You're a piano player?" she asks.

I glance around to make sure she's actually talking to me. "Yeah. I am. You play violin?"

"Yes. Since I was six. You?"

"Around there."

"Do you hate it?"

I blink. "What? No."

"I do," she replies, unfazed by my reaction. She piles her long black hair high on her head in a wild bun. "I can't stand it. I only played to make my parents happy and now I'm here, still trying to make them happy."

"What would you rather be doing?"

"I don't know." She smiles. "Anything else in the world."

"Then why don't you?"

"I told you. I'm trying to make my parents happy."

"Don't you want to be happy?"

"Yes. And I will be when they're happy because that's when the money starts coming in."

I shift in my seat uncomfortably. "Your family is rich?"

"Yours isn't?"

"No."

She scrunches her nose up. "Scholarships?"

I shake my head. "Student loans."

"Ouch!" she laughs. "That's even worse."

"Heather!" Asper calls from down the hall. He appears in the doorway, frowning at her. "Do you hear yourself?"

"No. Why?"

"You're being a bitch."

"I am not!"

Asper looks me dead in the eyes. "She sounded bitchy, didn't she?"

"About the scholarship and loan stuff? Yeah," I tell Heather bluntly, "you were coming off a little bitchy."

"I'm sorry!" she exclaims, looking honestly contrite. "I don't think about stuff before I say it. I would work on it but I don't want to."

"Still sounding bitchy," Asper calls, disappearing back down the hall.

Heather rolls her eyes. "Like I care what that queen thinks."

"He's gay?" I ask disbelieving.

"I don't know. Probably. Do you have a boyfriend?"

"Um, kind of."

"Kind of is not a yes." She jumps up off the couch, reaching for my hand. "Let's go to a bar. Get shit faced and hit on guys."

"Kind of is kind of, as in yeah, I sort of do, so no. I'm not going to hit on guys."

"Come get a drink anyway. You can watch me hit on guys."

I look at her standing there short and whisper thin with her wild hair and careless face and I think that watching her work a room will definitely be more fun than watching people learn to live in toolsheds with Asper.

"Alright, but I'm watching," I remind her as I stand. "Not participating."

She shrugs. "Whatever."

That turns out to be Heather's opinion on anything and everything. Whatever. The bouncer at the first bar thinks her ID is a fake (because it is) – whatever. A guy at the second bar won't buy her another drink even after she laughed at his accent – whatever. I want to go home and call it a night so my ass isn't dragging on the first day of classes tomorrow – whatever. That's the first one that really annoys me. I can't exactly leave her out at the bars alone, especially after she's been drinking and I'm dead sober, so I stay. I stay until after midnight. Until last call. Until I'm pushing her into a cab and asking if she has money to help pay it. Nope. No she doesn't.

For a rich girl she's quite the freeloader.

CHAPTER TWENTY-THREE

Morning comes too soon. I literally fall out of bed when my alarm goes off. Note to self – do not put the nightstand so far away. I overreach, slip off my sheets, and land face first on the floor. And I still consider going back to sleep once I'm down there.

When I'm dressed and my hair is half brushed I shuffle blearily toward the kitchen to see if I have any cereal left. I have to run to the grocery store today but after paying for a twenty three dollar cab ride last night I wonder how much I should really buy. I don't start my job at the coffee shop down the street until next week and while I still have a little money left over from the summer, I don't have much. And I don't want to touch my bonus. It sits in my savings like a safety net. A reminder that I can go home if I have to. If I can't stand not to.

"Morning," Asper greets me from the tiny kitchen. He's taking up most of it with his tall, gangly body and super low-cut white V-neck. He has a thin gray scarf around his neck, his black glasses that I'm pretty sure he doesn't need, and a matching gray skull cap pushed back far on his head.

Maybe I'm just exhausted but I'm a little jealous of how together his outfit looks. I had

Heather's 'whatever' attitude about getting dressed this morning, throwing on the same pair of capris I wore last night, a red tank, and a pair of black flip flops. Bam! Elegance achieved.

"Morning," I mumble.

"Do you want coffee?"

I hesitate, not sure if I do. Coffee is expensive. I haven't bought coffee since I got here and I definitely haven't used any in the apartment. Not since Heather used Molly's milk and we all woke up the next morning to carefully printed labels on everyone's food.

"Um, I would love some but…"

Asper grins. "But you're afraid of the consequences?"

"I fear the label maker."

"Here." He pours a mug full of black gold and slides it toward me over the counter. "You look like hell. You need this. Besides it's mine, and I give you full permission to drink it."

"I love you," I whisper, pulling the cup to my mouth.

He grimaces. "You drink it black?"

"I didn't buy coffee so I didn't buy cream or sugar."

"That is a sad story."

"Stick around. I'm full of 'em."

"Is that my mug?" Molly asks from directly behind me.

"Jesus gypsies!" I cry, nearly jumping through the roof. I spin around to face her, my heart lying dead flat on the floor. She looks at me emptily with her dark brown eyes, her thick red bangs hanging low over them. "You scared me, Molly."

"It is my mug," she mutters quietly.

She walks out of the kitchen silently, opens the front door, and glares at me as she closes it slowly behind her.

"Oooh," Asper chuckles quietly. "You just made her shit list."

"You gave me coffee in *her* mug?" I ask incredulously.

"I didn't know it was hers."

I look down at it, turn it in my hand, and sure enough, there it is on the front plain as day; Molly's name.

"Oh dammit."

Asper takes it from me and tosses the remains down the sink. "I'm sure she won't kill you in your sleep for using her mug."

"I'm not. Girl is intense."

"Come on." He waves for me to follow him. "We better get going if we want to be to class on time. We'll stop and get you some garlic to hang over your door on the way home."

I grab my bag, following him out the door. "It was her copy of Twilight, wasn't it?"

He smirks. "Sure as shit wasn't mine."

I feel myself smiling up at him. "Asper, I think I misjudged you when we met."

He looks me up and down, taking in my simple, casual outfit. "California, I had you dead to rights."

The first few days of class are pretty standard. It's a lot of lecture. A lot of syllabus review and clarification on how we'll be graded. You'd think that going to a music school classes would be very hands on. That everyone sits at their instrument and we play for hours on end, but that's not how it works. You don't go to medical school and immediately start operating on people. First you have to learn the history. The structure. The how's and why's of the way it works. Learning to play an instrument on your own is one thing, but getting used to the experience of playing with an orchestra or even with another person on another instrument, that's different. It takes a different kind of focus and awareness.

This is the part I've been afraid of. Finding out how good I am stacked up against other artists, and a few weeks later when I play with another pianist for the first time I get clarification on my skill level.

I'm not good.

In fairness, I'm not good compared to the raven-haired professor with the graying temples that I play with, which is like doing a finger painting next to Van Gogh and complaining that you suck. Of course you do. It's fucking Van Gogh.

"You were good enough to get in," Katy reminds me when I call her later that night. "They saw your talent and potential. That's why you're there. If you were as good as the professor on the first day what would be the point of even going to the school?"

"That's a good point," I admit. "But it didn't feel like the other students who played with him were as bumbling as I was."

"Maybe you were just nervous."

"I did feel like I was going to throw up."

"And maybe they weren't as good as you think

they were. Or you weren't as bad as you think. Who's your harshest critic?"

"Me."

"Exactly. I'm sure you were fine," she assures me. "Did the professor say anything when you were done?"

"No."

"Then don't worry."

"He complimented the other students."

Katy hesitates. "All of them?"

"Every last one."

"Damn."

"Yup."

"Okay, well," Katy rallies, "it's only been a month. You'll get better and you'll get that compliment from him."

"What if I don't get better?"

"Then he isn't a very good teacher."

I smile at her buoyancy. Her unrelenting optimism. It's one of the things I've always loved so much about Katy.

"You should be a teacher," I tell her. "You've got the attitude for it."

"Do you think?"

"Absolutely."

"'Cause I've thought about that before."

"Seriously?"

"Yeah," she says shyly. "I've looked into what it takes to be a kindergarten teacher. I've even shadowed Mrs. Halpert at our old school to see how I'd like it. She's like a hundred years old now and ready to retire soon."

"You should do it," I tell her adamantly. "You

have to do it."

"Do you think?" she asks hesitantly.

"I've never been more sure of anything. That is such a better job for you than the grocery store."

She laughs. "Anything is better than the grocery store."

"Promise me you'll do it. That you'll look into classes."

"I will, but only if you promise me you'll give yourself a break and remember you're there to learn, not blow everybody away on your first day."

"I promise."

"Me too."

We fall into a lull in the conversation and I do everything I can to not fill it with questions about Lawson. I want to ask a million things. I want to know everything he's doing and who he's doing it with, but I can't. If I find out he's dating someone I'll be crushed and if I find out he's not I'll be desperate to come home to be with him.

"Wyatt kissed me again."

I sit up straight on my bed. "When?"

"Last weekend at a beach party."

"Those are still going on?"

"Endless summer, baby," she reminds me, a smile in her tone.

"How'd it go?"

"The party?"

"The kiss."

"Oh, you know," she sighs dramatically. "Standard panty dropper."

"Did you…"

"No!" she exclaims. "Dude, come on. I'm still

getting over Aaron."

"Fastest way to get over a guy—"

"Is to get under another, I know. I know. It's very clever. It's also not true."

"I know."

"I like him, though," she says quietly. "Wyatt. He's a sweet guy."

"I've always thought so."

"Baker too."

I laugh. "He's alright, I guess."

"They're all alright. *All* of them," she insists meaningfully. "They're good. And they hope you're good too."

I feel my throat constrict tightly and suddenly it's hard to breathe. It's hard to be. "That's—it's really good to hear." I cough roughly, standing up and pacing my room. "I gotta go, okay? But I'll call you tomorrow?"

"I'll be here."

"Thanks, Katy. And hey," I add quickly, my heart racing. "Tell them... tell them I miss them, okay?"

"I will."

When I hang up the phone I have to stand there for a minute breathing evenly. The tears eventually stop trying to well in my eyes and I'm able to move again. I'm able to put my phone down, pick my notebook up, and sit at my desk to study, because as much as I want to replay the last part of the conversation with Katy over and over again in my mind, I don't. I can't. That's not why I'm here.

TRACEY WARD

CHAPTER TWENTY-FOUR

My first term ends and I'm drained. I'm spent emotionally and mentally. I worked my ass off but I never got that compliment from my professor. In fact, after finals he asks me into his office to 'have a talk'. Those words have never preceded anything good. Never.

"Sit down, Miss Mason," he commands, gesturing to the hard wooden chair across from his cluttered desk.

The room is dark, the shades partially drawn to block out the last of the early evening light. It's the start of December and the sun sets around four these days. We're lucky to get nine hours of daylight and while I know California is getting the same amount of sun, the quality is definitely different. I'm bundled up against the cold that's been dropping steadily into the thirties and forties while I'm sure everyone back home is still in shorts and flip flops, enjoying the seventy degree heat.

"It's Rachel," I tell him, getting settled. "If you don't mind."

He smiles faintly. "I don't."

"Did you want to talk to me about my test?"

"No. I want to talk to you about your audition tape."

"Oh," I reply numbly, taken aback. "What about it?"

"How often did you practice those pieces?" He consults a note on his desk. "Dohnanyi's Concert Etude #6, Gershwin's Piano Prelude #1, Bach's French Suite #4, and Liszt's Années de Pèlerinage."

"Every day."

"Every day," he repeats thoughtfully. He puts his note down, sitting back in his seat to observe me. "I don't doubt it. I reviewed your tape just last night and you were good. Very clean, precise."

"Thank you."

"Was that your first audition?"

I feel myself start to flush with embarrassment. "No."

"You applied before with the same pieces, I assume?"

"Yes."

"How long did you wait between applications?"

"Two years. I applied while I was still in high school." I spread my hands helplessly. "I was denied. Then I spent two years practicing, I applied again last January, and I was accepted."

"Do you know why you were accepted?"

"Because I showed promise?" I ask slowly.

He shakes his head. "No, because you showed talent. You had four pieces learned down to a science. You could probably play them in your sleep."

"I think I do."

"Yes. But what else can you play with that level of skill?"

I open my mouth to answer but nothing comes out. I close it, try again, and still nothing. Finally I answer with just that; "Nothing."

"So I've seen," he agrees bluntly. "I won't lie, you're a very good pianist. Very expressive and reasonably well trained."

"Reasonably well trained?"

Is he talking about me or a border collie who occasionally shits on the rug?

"I do believe, however, that you've done yourself and the school a disservice by repeating your audition pieces."

"There were no rules against it."

"No, there aren't, but audition tapes are difficult to judge. We prefer live performance because believe me, if you'd performed in front of me I would have asked you exactly what I'm asking you now. I would insist you play something new. I would have encouraged you to choose a piece off the cuff and judged your talent by your ability to adapt. By the depth of your arsenal. As it appears, you have no arsenal. You possess but four bullets in your chamber. Hardly what it takes to go to war."

"I thought the point of coming here was to gather more bullets. More weapons. I thought the entire point was for you to teach me how to be better," I argue, my temper flaring.

"And I can. I could. You'd get better than you are now, but I have to ask you what your end game is. Where do you see yourself in four years?"

I already know where this is going. What he's going to say, and I take a steadying breath before I speak to keep from shouting at him. "The Boston

Philharmonic."

"No."

"Fine. I'd go home. The Los Angeles Philharmonic."

"No."

I breathe again, deep and slow. "Do you want me to name every orchestra in the country or should we cut to the chase?"

He nods, sitting forward to put his elbows on his desk. "I'll teach you. Every professor here will teach you and we'll do our best to refine your talent, because I strongly agree that you do have talent, but what you don't have is the *right* kind of talent. You're creative. Dreamy. You're not disciplined. You're not concise, meaning you're not orchestra material, and if that's your goal in all of this I feel it's important to warn you of it now."

"You think I should drop out?"

"I think you should give stark consideration to your future. A law student who has no head for facts will never be a lawyer. He'll spend a lot of time and money on school, but he'll never get hired. He'll never pass the bar. If being a lawyer is his dream, he'd better find himself a new dream." He raises his eyebrows at me, thick and bushy. Like crooked spined caterpillars. "Do you understand what I'm saying?"

I stand abruptly, snatching up my bag from the floor. "I'm undisciplined, not dumb. Thank you for your time and words of wisdom."

He doesn't respond to my outburst. He lets me leave, hurrying out of the room as fast as I can go. I nearly run down the long hall toward the exit. I burst through the thick double doors and into the cold that stings my eyes. It pierces my last defenses until I crack. Until I try to breathe in deeply but my lungs fight against the frigid air and I cough, hiccup, and burst into tears that spill hot down my chilled cheeks.

I nearly run home, my head down and my burning face hidden under my hair. It looks so dark in the coming night. More brown than blond and I choke on a sob that climbs up the back of my throat and reaches greedily for my lips.

I just want to be alone. I want to cry and get over it and move on, but I'm shit out of luck. The second I step inside they all look up at me. Asper from the couch, Heather from the kitchen, and Molly from her laptop at the dining table. I hesitate, door open behind me, and I consider going back outside. But my phone is here and I have to call Katy. I have to call someone and more than anything on this earth I want to call Lawson, to have him pull me through the phone to the other side where the sun is shining and the beach is frothing. Where his skin is warm and gritty from the sand. Where my scars are beautiful and my heart is home.

"What happened?" Asper asks, concern creasing his brow. "Are you okay?"

I wipe at my face and close the door behind me. "Yeah, I'm fine."

"You're crying," Molly points out.

"I know."

Heather leans against the counter with interest. "Why?"

"It's private."

"Oh come on, we don't keep secrets here."

"You mean *you* don't," Asper corrects. "The rest of us do. It's called privacy. Now let her have it."

Heather rolls her eyes. "We all know what your secret is."

"I only have one?"

"You're gay. Get over yourself. No one cares."

Asper laughs in amazement. "I'm not gay!"

"I am," Molly says in her perfect monotone.

We all look at her for half a second before Heather starts to laugh.

"What do you mean, you're not gay?" she demands of Asper. "I call bullshit!"

"What have I ever done that made you think I was gay?" he spits back.

"Um, only everything? You wear Mr. Rogers sweaters, your underwear always matches your socks—"

"How the hell do you know that?!"

"And you haven't hit on me even once since you got here." She points at him accusingly. "Gay!"

"Sorry to break it to you, but I'm straight as an arrow, and the reason I haven't hit on you is because you're a rich bitch and I don't care how hot your body is, your personality is repulsive."

"Hey, you guys," I say slowly, looking between the two of them, "let's take it easy."

"Whatever," Heather barks at him, steaming down the hall.

She slams her door, making Asper and I jump slightly. Molly keeps clicking away on her keyboard like nothing happened.

"So, I'm gonna... head to my room for... just for a bit to... yeah," I tell the room awkwardly, not even sure who I'm talking to or what I said.

I spin on my heel and hurry back to my bedroom, closing the door and resting my forehead against it. I stare at my feet on the floor, blinking rapidly, replaying what just happened in my head.

I'm surprised as shit when I start to laugh instead of cry.

***

Almost a week later and I haven't told anyone anything. Not my roommates, not my family, and not even Katy. I'm still trying to sort it out. I want to know how I feel about it before I tell anyone, and that bit – my feelings – is what has me confused.

I'm not sad.

I cried when my professor told me I wasn't good enough to be in an orchestra, but it was more humiliation than anything else. When I really thought about it, when I lay down that night to sleep, what I felt was relief. It's the shark bite all over again. It comes with a freeing sense of euphoria. A weight lifted from my shoulders.

I'm not good enough.

End of story.

So what do I do now?

"Hey," Asper says quietly. "You're still up?"

He's standing in my doorway in his pajamas (full fucking pajamas with lapels and everything), his hands on the frame and his body leaning inside.

His glasses are off and his hair is casually mussed. A little too casually to be real. But his face is open and earnest and I find myself smiling at him from my seat at my desk.

"Yeah, I can't sleep."

"Me either. I've gotta take Molly to the airport in the morning. My ass is gonna be dragging."

"Where is she from?"

"Mars as far as I can tell."

I stifle a laugh, careful not to get too loud and wake up Sleeping Beauty across the hall. Heather and Asper haven't spoken since their fight. I've never seen Asper so relaxed.

"You're not going home for Christmas?" he asks, but he knows I'm not. I'm the only one who isn't. Day after tomorrow I'll be alone in the apartment for the next three weeks. Through Christmas and New Year's.

"No," I reply, shaking my head. "Can't afford it. I'll be here watching Christmas specials and eating all of Molly's sugar cubes."

"God, that's depressing."

"That's the holidays."

"What about the guy?"

I shrug. "What guy?"

"Don't act dumb. You know the guy. The one you don't talk about."

"How do you know about him if I don't talk about him?"

"Because he sent you that package. Lawson, right?"

My back goes stiff. "What package? Where is it?"

He frowns. "You don't have it?"

"No."

He turns and goes into the kitchen with me close on his heels. He looks around, spinning in circles and retracing steps I don't know, but he comes up empty. Then his shoulders slump.

"She's unbelievable," he groans.

"Who?"

He storms down the hall, passing me quickly. "One guess."

I'm shocked when he throws open Heather's door. He flicks on the light and starts rooting through piles of clothes that cover every surface.

Heather sits up in her bed slowly, blinking against the light.

"What's happening?" she moans.

"Where is it, Heather?" Asper demands. He tosses a hot pink thong at her face before toppling a pile of skirts to the floor.

She glares at him with a pout, then turns her angry stare to me. "Will you please remind that asshole that I'm not speaking to him and will you tell him to get the hell out of my room?!"

"Not until you tell me where the box is," he tells her hotly. "The one I told you to give to Rachel."

"Rachel, please tell the asshole I don't remember anything and I won't remember anything until I get an apology."

"Heather, where is it?" I ask her urgently.

She shrugs, looking away like a petulant child. "I don't what you're talking about. No one gave me a box. Must have been a ghost."

I move in close, leaning over the bed on my knuckles and putting my face up to hers until she can't look away. Until I'm in her eyes and her space. "You better tell me where that box is," I warn her softly, "or the only ghost around here will be you, do you understand me? I'm from Cali, bitch. You don't wanna fuck with me."

She's all talk. Pure bravado and attitude used to hiding behind her daddy and his money that crumbles under my stare.

"Top shelf of the closet," she tells me quickly, her eyes tight and worried.

Asper steps over more mess and reaches for the shelf. He pulls down a small cardboard box with brown packaging tape around the outside. Tape that's been cut.

"She opened it," he tells me, handing it over.

I turn to look at Heather, but she shakes her head hard. "It's all there. I didn't take anything. I just looked. He's hot. Congrats."

I don't respond. I leave the room and head across the hall for mine, hearing Asper mutter a curse at her as he follows me.

I put the box on my bed and take a step back, watching it. Waiting for it to move. To tell me what to do, but it doesn't have to because I already know. I knew before I found it.

"What's in it?" Asper asks, back to leaning in my doorway.

"I don't know."

"Do you want some privacy to open it?"

"No," I answer instantly. "I want something else. A favor."

"Sure. What do you need?"

I turn and throw open my closet. I pull my suitcase out and toss it open on the bed next to the box.

"A ride to the airport tomorrow," I tell him decidedly. "I'm going home."

CHAPTER TWENTY-FIVE

I don't open the box until I'm in the air. Until I've boarded the plane and I'm allowed to play Candy Crush on my phone for the next five hours. But I don't. Instead I pull the brown box from my carry on and I set it on the tray in front of me. The flight is light, not many passengers, and there's no one next to me. No one to see me read the return address on the label. To see me smile faintly when I read the city.

Malibu.

He got out, I think happily.

Inside is a jersey. A bright red surfer's jersey with the words 'Cascais Billabong' written across the stomach and 'WSL' just under the collar. It takes me a second to remember why I know that name, Cascais, but then it hits me. Portugal. Lawson competed in the Cascais Billabong Pro in Portugal.

Did he win?

I pull the satiny material of the jersey into my lap and dive inside the box. There's a postcard with a picture of a gorgeous, rocky beach on the front and the words 'Wish you were here' scribbled across the back with a small heart in the corner. I smile at it before pulling out the only thing left in the box – a picture. It's of Lawson and three other guys standing on a podium. He's wearing the red jersey. He's smiling and gorgeous, totally natural under the attention of a crowd of strangers in a foreign country. The guy next to him is holding up a trophy while Lawson and the third guy wave to the crowd. He obviously didn't win, not first place, but he must have taken second or third. My money is on second.

I flip the picture over hopefully. He doesn't let me down.

There's a note penned across the back.

Second place ain't bad.

"Called it," I sing to myself quietly.

Got out of my backyard. You were right. It's better out here.

I reread it three times, still smiling and so proud and happy for him that I'm nearly bursting. I wish I could use my phone to look up the rankings online. The season is over, but I want to know – did he stay in the top sixteen? Did he qualify for the World Tour next year?

It's another four and a half hours before I can find out.

***

He didn't make it.

I stare in disbelief at my phone as I wait for the luggage carousel to start spinning and spit out my stuff, but the numbers don't change. He wasn't even in the top twenty, let alone the top sixteen.

His numbers disappeared after the two events in Portugal that he attended. He placed in the second one, though not as highly as the first, and with no more competitions under his belt for the rest of the year he couldn't keep up with the growing scores of the other competitors. They were still traveling, hitting up Japan and Tahiti. Hawaii and Brazil while Lawson apparently stayed home. I wonder if it had anything to do with his brother.

The room bursts into action as yellow lights flash, a monotone alarm sounds, and the belt starts to weave its path in front of me. I watch it go, feeling mesmerized.

I could call him. I could call my parents or Katy. I probably should. I haven't told anyone I'm home. I've gotten into the habit of not talking to people about how I feel or what I'm doing. It feels weird to think about calling Lawson, though. To hear his voice on the phone and not in person. But am I going to Malibu? It'd be smarter to head home on the bus toward Santa Barbara. I would bypass Malibu all together.

It's what I *should* do, but is it what I want to do? When am I going to start doing what I want and not what I should?

"Today," I whisper to myself

The old woman standing next to me at the luggage carousel glances over uneasily.

I smile at her, probably a little maniacally, and sweep my bag off the belt as it slips by.

I hurry out the doors into the cool early morning air of a southern California winter. I have a coat on but it's unbuttoned. No mittens, no scarves. No frostbite. It's heaven. It's everything that's right with the world and nothing that was wrong with

Boston. If any part of me doubted coming home was the right choice, it shuts the hell up right then and there.

And when I get on a bus to Malibu, it starts to sing.

When the bus drops me off I take a cab to the ocean front condominium at the return address on the box. I leave my suitcase with the man at the small desk by the elevators, telling him I'm there to see Lawson Daniel.

"I'll call him and let him know you're here," he tells me, reaching for the phone.

I put my hand out to stop him. "He won't be up there."

"Oh. How do you know?"

"Because I know him," I reply with a grin. "I know where he is."

When I reach the beach on the other side of the building I'm not surprised to find I'm right. He's there on the horizon waiting for a wave, his legs in the water on either side of Layla. It's such a familiar sight that it takes my breath away and replaces it with something else. Something warm and full that sits heavily in my body until I've sunk down into the sand.

I sit and watch him surf the way I used to in the early morning. It's cooler now. Softer and gentler than it was in the summer heat. It feels more comfortable than it ever has and I think it's because I know it's right this time. I went out, I tried the world, and I found it lacking. Nothing on this earth can feel as good as being home for me. Nothing can ever be as good as him.

He takes two waves before he spots me, but when he does his reaction is immediate. He comes to shore instantaneously, riding Layla as far as she'll carry him and then he's running with her up the beach. I smile, standing to greet him, but I'm not ready for the force of his embrace when it comes. His hug takes my legs out from under me, his body knocking me backward so hard I'm clinging to him to stay upright and he's laughing and wet and strong. He's holding me up as he's knocking me down and I giggle against his shoulder like a little kid.

"You're back?" he asks breathily, his mad sprint from the water taking its toll on his voice.

I nod my head against him, his wet hair dripping down into mine. Onto my smiling face. "I'm back."

He leans back, not letting me go. "When? When did you get back?"

"A little over an hour ago."

"For how long?"

"Forever."

I feel his body literally soften with relief. "What happened?"

"I failed," I chuckle lightly.

He grins. "Me too."

"We're a couple of losers, aren't we?"

Lawson laughs, reaching up to push my windblown hair from my eyes. "You're *my* loser."

"Are you still mine?"

"Always, Rach. I'll always be your loser."

He leans down to kiss me softly, sweetly, and then I'm in his arms again. I'm pressed against him

TRACEY WARD

with my face to the ocean and the sun on my skin and I can't even remember what it was like to not be here with him. It's like the tide has already taken the memory away, sifting it with the sand, dispersing it with the grains until it's lost and unrecognizable.

"Congratulations on Portugal," I tell him quietly.

"You got your present?"

"I did. I love it."

"I lost the second one."

"I know. But you tried."

He kisses the top of my head. "So did you."

"They told me I'm good but not good enough."

"Ouch."

"It was the best news I've gotten since I found out I still had my leg."

He chuckles silently, holding me close. The only sound is the roar of the ocean that's on his skin and seeping into mine. "I'm gonna try again."

"Good. I'm glad."

He hesitates. "Will you?"

"No," I answer honestly. "I don't want to. I know what I am and I know what I'm not now. I'm not a concert pianist, I'm a mixed tape. I don't belong anywhere in the world but where I'm happy and California makes me happy." I squeeze him hard. "You make me happy."

"I'm gonna be gone a lot if I make another run at the World Tour."

"I know."

"Where will you be when I come back?"

I lean back, shaking my head, unsure what he's

asking. "I'll be here."

"Here in Malibu?"

"No."

"Why not?" he asks frankly. "Don will hire you again. He'll probably pay you better than before since you're showing loyalty by coming back."

"I can't afford to live in Malibu, even with a raise."

"I know a place you could afford."

I laugh. "You always know a guy or a place or a band, don't you?"

"I get around."

"So I've heard."

He lowers his brow playfully. "Ooh, low blow, Mason."

I stand up on my toes to kiss him. "Now you're being a tease," I whisper.

I can feel him smiling against my lips. "Rachel."

"Mmmm," I hum, savoring the sound of my name in his deep tenor. It rolls through my body like warm honey, making me sinuous and sweet.

"My apartment is big," he tells me quietly. "And lonely."

"You should get a dog," I joke.

"I don't want a dog. I want you."

"You have me." I kiss him again, dying to get closer.

He leans away from me, taking his mouth out of reach. His eyes are serious and so, so green. "What do you say?"

I blink. "To what exactly? What are we talking about, Lawson?"

"You moving in with me."

"I—" I begin, unsure how to finish that sentence. "You want me to live with you?"

"Yeah. I'll be gone a lot during the season, but I would love to come home to you every break." He leans in again, making me soft. "So, what do you say?

I should think it through. I should talk to my parents about it. I should talk to Don first and make sure I'd actually have a job down here. I should at least ask what my share of the rent would be, but I don't. Instead I ask myself what I *want*, tapping into my heart and not my head, and I know immediately, beyond a shadow of a doubt.

"Yes," I tell him with a smile. "I say yes."

Lawson glows happily as he leans in to kiss me. I let myself melt in his arms, into the sand, and when he pulls me toward the building to show me upstairs I'm on a cloud. I ride with him high up into the building to his condo with his hand in mine, his thumb running absently over my skin.

The place is amazing, all white walls and marble countertops. It doesn't feel much like Lawson, though, and he's quick to explain that it came furnished. Nothing here is really his.

He gives me a tour that ends in the living room looking out large windows that frame the ocean outside. It's there that we stop, that the world stops, and we disappear from it for the next hour. I ask to see his scars, the ones he promised to show me in the hospital, and he grins that crooked, knowing grin of his before he agrees.

Lawson shows me slowly. It starts with his leg

and ends with his clothes on the floor and my lips on his skin, tasting each story his body tells me the way he tasted mine. Seeing him, all of him. The truth and the lies, the rumors and the reality, and showing him every piece of me that I've never had the courage to share. My honesty. My whole heart, so full to bursting with him and the warmth of the sun that I'm near tears when his body finally finds mine. When our stories come together and the only truth that matters is this.

Is us.

EPILOGUE

"This summer's gonna be another scorcher," Lawson comments.

I watch as he lifts Layla off the stand by the front door, the muscles on his back flexing and rolling under his tan skin. I know it's all in my head but his skin looks darker than I've ever seen it. All that foreign sunlight giving him a deeper hue.

He got back late last night from Hawaii but the week before he'd been in Brazil. Two weeks before that he was in Japan. He brings me something small and touristy from every place he visits – a keychain, a magnet, a little figurine. I have a collection starting on the wall by the door with the date he came home written on the back of each one. I see it every time I leave the apartment, every time I come inside, and it makes me smile to know that even though he's not here, he's coming back. He always comes back to me.

"I can handle a hot summer as long as I have air conditioning," I tell him from the kitchen.

I live in peace in the cold air inside the condo knowing my parents are feeling the relief as well. I convinced them to sell the piano they got me for Christmas and buy a new air conditioner for the house. They weren't thrilled about it first. Not until earlier this month when the heat wave started. Now they're all smiles.

"You're letting that sausage cook too long," Lawson warns me.

"Shit," I mutter. I flip it over and see that he's right. It's getting charred on one side. "How did you know that?!"

"I was timing it."

"You're a friggin' witch, is what happened," I whisper.

"I heard that."

"I stand by it! You should not have been able to hear that."

He comes to stand across the counter from me, smiling at my anger. "You're not as quiet as you think you are."

"Maybe I wasn't trying."

"Maybe."

I kill the heat on the stove, giving up. "Will you please make the sandwich for me?"

"Nope. You said you wanted to be able to make them when I'm gone. You've gotta learn how."

"Dude, please," I plead pathetically. "I'm so hungry."

He shakes his head, his smile widening. "You're mom learned how to make them on one try."

"Well, she's amazing."

"So are you. Keep trying."

"Ugh!"

He laughs as he grabs a grape out of the bowl on the counter. "What time do you work today?"

"I don't. Don gave me the day off since you're

home. Do you want to go into the shop anyway?"

"Yeah, after I hit the surf. I need to talk to him about Tahiti."

"Are you gonna go?"

"I don't know if I need to."

"But do you want to?"

He shrugs. "It'd be killer, but if I don't have to so why do it?"

"Practice. Prize money. Fame. Glory."

"Only one of those sounds appealing."

I wipe my hands on a towel and toss it near the sink. "You should go."

"You should go with me."

I roll my eyes. "Uh uh, no. One a year, we agreed."

"Two. I'm still pushing for two."

"Maybe next year. This year I want to do the World Tour event with you."

Lawson is going back to Portugal. While he didn't earn himself an invite to compete in the World Tour for the championship, he did impress the people in Cascais who organized the Billabong Pro. So much so that they invited him back, giving him a wildcard invite to compete. He won't earn any points, he can't possibly win the championship title, but it's a good opportunity to get experience on the tour against the guys who made it. And any prize money he earns is his to keep.

When he started making his schedule for the year he asked me to go to at least four events with him. That's a lot. It's a lot of time away from work, time traveling, and a lot of expense. It's easy for Lawson to go because it's his job. He makes good money when he wins or places and his sponsors pay him well to make the appearances.

All of his boards, once clean and devoid of any emblems or stickers, now all sport a very distinctive red A and a simple yellow and black emblem that reads 'Dee's Wax'.

While I was away Lawson went to Don for advice on diving into the qualifying tour. In addition to advice and an offer to mentor him, Don offered him sponsorships. One from Ambrose Surf and another from the board wax business he's part owner in. Lawson and Don's partner agreed and there was a small press conference in Florida at the Dee's Wax headquarters where Lawson signed with both companies. Suddenly the sky was the limit on his travel, he was renting his condo from Don for a song, and he had one of the most adored men in surfing history backing his play. That's when the wildcard came in and since then Lawson has exploded all over the surfing scene. He was well known in California and by a few of the pros who competed against him when they came here, but his face is international now. Guys in Australia and Africa are watching out for him, studying his competition footage and getting a feel for what they're up against.

A whirlwind, that's what.

"You could go to both," Lawson suggests.

"I have to work."

"Not really."

"Don't start that again," I warn him.

Lawson doesn't charge me rent. He grudgingly accepts help with utilities, and if he got this way I would quit my job at Ambrose and spend the year traveling to events with him. I can't do it, though. I gave up on playing piano in an orchestra because it's not what I wanted, but I'm not looking to lose myself entirely. I've joined a small band with three other girls, playing keyboard and just jamming on the weekends. We have no goals, no dreams of making it big. We play to play, that's all there is to it, and I've never loved piano more. I've never played this way before – wild and untethered. It feels like the way Lawson surfs. Following a rhythm where it takes me. No rules, no expectations. Only a feeling. Freedom. I'm addicted to it and if I quit everything to follow Lawson around the world I'd have to give that up too, and I won't do it.

"I know, I'm sorry," he relents, stepping back from the counter.

I soften my tone. "It's not that I don't want to go."

"I know. I get it, though. I'll back off."

"Thank you."

He grins at me, quirking his eyebrow high.

"What?" I ask.

He doesn't answer. Only looks at me disapprovingly.

I pick up the towel and throw it at him. "Let it go!"

"No way," he laughs. "It's still fun."

"I'm gonna start leaving you Thank You cards in your suitcase when you go. Thank you for leaving your dirty underwear on the bathroom floor for me to pick up. Thank you for drinking ninety-nine point nine percent of the milk and putting the dredges back in the fridge."

"Thank you for rocking my world last night," he throws out with a grin.

"You're welcome."

"I meant—"

"I know what you meant. Oh!" I pick up my phone, checking the calendar. "Remember, you have a date with Aaron tomorrow."

He cringes. "Don't call it a date. It sounds weird."

"What do you want me to call it?"

"An awkward lunch in a dark room?"

"He's making progress," I protest. "He's been in L.A. for almost a year, and he and your mom are looking at apartments next week. That's huge for him."

"I know," Lawson agrees tiredly. "I get that he's doing better but it's still exhausting going over there. He still won't talk about anything that happened before the accident. It's like he made huge strides after talking to Katy and now he's backsliding."

"He's working on it."

"Yeah. Hey," he says, his tone lightening immediately as he changes the subject and the feel of the room, "if I make you that sandwich will you surf with me today?"

"Baby, if you make me breakfast I will do anything you want."

He laughs, coming around the counter. "That's a bold promise."

"I'm counting on you being a gentleman."

"You obviously don't know me very well."

I hug him from behind, my cheek on his back and his heartbeat hollow and strong in my ear.

"I know you," I promise him affectionately. "I see you, Lawson Daniel, even if no one else does."

"And what do you see?"

"I see the ocean in your eyes."

He chuckles, jostling us both gently. "Oh yeah?"

"Yes."

"I know you too, Rachel Mason."

"What do you know?"

He turns to face me, pulling me close. His lips hover over mine, only a breath away but still too far. "I hear the music in your heart," he whispers.

"So sappy," I laugh. "You must be tired."

"Among other things."

I back up, pointing to my unfinished breakfast. "Sandwich first."

"Surfing first," he counters.

"Sandwich before surfing."

"Those are your priorities? Sandwich, surfing, sex?"

"Yours are surfing then sex!" I exclaim. "Why are you judging my sandwich?"

He pauses, debating. "Sex, sandwich, surfing, sex."

I smile. "That's a sex sandwich."

"This conversation is becoming a tongue twister."

"Sally sells sex sandwiches in the surf shop by the seashore."

"Rachel?" Lawson laughs.

"Yeah?"

"I love you."

I smile, stripping my shirt off over my head and stepping into his arms, my hunger put on hold. "I love you too, Lawson."

ABOUT THE AUTHOR

I was born in Eugene, Oregon and studied English Literature at the University of Oregon (Go Ducks!) I love writing all kinds of genres from YA Dystopian to New Adult Romance, the common themes between them all being strong character development and a good dose of humor. My husband, son, and snuggly pitbull are my world.

Visit my website for more information on upcoming releases, www.traceywardauthor.com